REPERCUSSIONS

ANTHEA HOLLAND

Published in 2009 by New Generation
Publishing

First Edition

For Jeff, the most important person in my life

And also for the most precious people in my life –

Angie, Martin and Kieron

With my love

CHAPTER ONE

The day I moved in it started to snow. It was late October, and the locals told me the snow had come late this year.

The house, an old brown-stone, was imposing. It had big rooms and an even bigger ego. In property terms, this house considered itself 'top of the heap'. Once upon a time a wealthy family probably lived here but I doubted that any families lived here now. I suspected that its residents were all singles - not quite down-and-outs but those unfortunates who were only a few steps above them on the ladder of life.

In front of the house was a sometimes-busy road, beyond which was a parking lot, flanked by diners and bars, hotels and the odd private dwelling. The house's surroundings didn't really bother me though, I didn't imagine that I would be gazing out at the view very much.

The room that I could just about afford to rent – as long as I didn't plan on doing anything frivolous, like eating – was a good size, but although it was listed as an "apartment", it was little more than a bed-sit. The only difference is that I had my own kitchen (minuscule) and my own shower room and toilet (even tinier). I would still have to go to the basement to do my laundry though, along with the other 27 residents.

Still, I was just glad to have somewhere I could call my own, and on the plus side it was within walking distance of the office, so I'd save on the cost of public transport.

I'd picked the keys up from the landlord's office on the other side of town and trudged through the falling flakes to my new home, wrapped up so well that only my eyes showed. The front door of the house was open and I lugged my two suitcases and one backpack up the stairs to the third story (no elevator! I hadn't noticed that on the viewing, but then I wasn't carrying all this luggage then!) and located my room. My fingers were numb despite the ski gloves that I had been wearing and I fumbled with the key in the lock for a while before it finally turned and I threw open the door.

And gasped.

When I'd viewed the room the previous week it had been late afternoon and the sunset had suffused the room with a red glow, making everything appear warm and cosy. Now the day was overcast and I could see the shabby room for what it really was. A dump. The plastic couch had rips on the arms from which stuffing was meandering down to the floor. The cupboards in the kitchen area were scratched and chipped and their surfaces stained by the dripping from numerous cups of caffeine-riddled tea and coffee, not to mention burnt saucepan bottoms.

I kicked aside a soiled rug and exposed a series of burns in the worn carpet on the floor. I was pretty sure that the small television in the corner wasn't going to work although it had held a picture when it was demonstrated to me on my previous visit and I doubted that the old radiator along one wall would give out much heat.

I noted all this in the time it took me to enter the room. Sighing, I put my cases down and flung the backpack on the sofa before closing the door and locking it from the inside. As an extra precaution I put the chain on and slid across the bolt that a previous resident had added to the door. I was locked up like Fort Knox and hoped that all this security didn't indicate that this was a neighbourhood in which a person was at risk from intruders. I didn't think it was, I'd asked around in the office and the general consensus of opinion was that it was a good area in which to live; a bit noisy on occasions in the evening with people coming and going to and from the diners and bars, but it was considered to have a relatively low crime rate. This was a fact that I felt was important for a woman on her own, especially one who was feeling vulnerable anyway.

I pulled out my cell 'phone, ready to rant and rave at my landlord who, incidentally, was a distant relative of my mother's. If I had thought that link would enable me to rent a room for a little less cost than normal then I had been sadly mistaken.

I hesitated. What was I going to say to him if I called? I'd seen the room the previous week and accepted it as it was. It wasn't Con's fault that I'd seen the room through rose tinted glasses. And no, the aptness of my mother's second-cousin-once-removed's name hadn't escaped me.

I put my cell 'phone back in my bag and instead I fumbled in my pocket and found some loose change with which to feed the meter, then I switched on the light and wandered round the room, running fingers across surfaces. I peeked into the shower room as I passed. At least the place was clean, that was something. I unwrapped my scarf and took off the woolly hat my mother had sent me from England and threw them on top of the cases.

It didn't take long to cover the floor space and when I got to the bed I pulled off the comforter and ripped the sheet from the mattress which was, of course, stained with – no, I didn't want to go there. Anyway, there was no way that I was going to sleep in someone else's sheets, even if they *did* look clean.

This was unreasonable, I knew. If I stayed in a hotel I slept in the sheets provided, didn't I? But this was my home and therefore had different rules.

I opened my suitcase and pulled out the ironed flannelette sheet. It was one of the few things that I had managed to hang on to, by spiriting it out of the apartment I had shared with Glen and getting a friend to look after it for me. In fact, the same friend was storing some table linen; there was no table here, so I didn't see the need to bring it with me, the room was going to be crowded enough as it was. Lucy was also hanging on to some clothes and shoes I'd salvaged; things I'd got out of the apartment I had shared with Glen before he could get his hands on them and flog them.

I made the bed up, shivering all the while. I'd checked the oil filled radiator and, as I'd suspected, even turned up high it wasn't throwing out enough heat to make much difference in the room.

The bed made, I hunted round the kitchen for a kettle. "Fully furnished and linen provided" the apartment details had said which, to my mind, should include a kettle, and I was sure there'd been one by the cooker hob when I'd inspected the place. There was nothing remotely resembling a kettle there now though. I pulled a rusty looking saucepan from the cupboard and let the tap run for a while, the tap clonking all the time, before rinsing out and filling the saucepan. I put the saucepan of water on the hob to boil and searched for something to drink from.

There were a couple of chipped mugs in the cupboard; the white insides of them stained a nicotine-brown. I didn't fancy drinking from either of them. Instead, I found an intact glass at the back of the cupboard which I rinsed out and into which I put a spoon – my mother had always recommended this if boiling water was going to be poured into a glass. I had a sudden longing to be a child again; tucked up in bed with a cold – nothing too serious, just ill enough to warrant a bit of pampering – and Mum bringing me a hot lemon squash.

I gave myself a mental shake, I should know better than to linger on thoughts of home.

Picking up the backpack I took out the coffee and sugar and arranged them on the shelves above the kitchen cupboards. Lucy had provided me with the bare essentials to get through the night; I'd have to go shopping tomorrow. The milk she'd given me I'd leave on the windowsill overnight. It would keep as cold there as it would in the 'fridge, and I didn't want to put anything actually *in* the 'fridge until I'd given it a good wash.

I made myself a black coffee, slung my coat on the sofa, found a notebook and pen in my backpack, pulled off my boots and climbed into bed. I should have dug out my pj's but I just couldn't be bothered.

Good grief! I now realised that at least I should have taken the time to find the hot water bottle that was in my suitcase. Too late now, I couldn't face the idea of getting out of bed again. I just hoped that it didn't take long for the bed to warm up.

I sipped my coffee and felt the warmth course through my chilled body, while I jotted down on the pad a list of things that I needed to pick up from the shops in the morning. I'd got a couple of days vacation from work and I wasn't totally penniless, although I didn't know how long my meagre savings would have to last, so I couldn't throw it away on unnecessary purchases.

Things like a new mattress would be luxuries, and therefore not an option, but I could replace the curtains, I supposed. The ones currently hanging at the windows were thin and frayed at the bottoms and sported rather a lot of holes. There was no double-glazing at the windows and some thick, lined curtains would help keep the cold at bay. Luckily I was a good seamstress and I knew where I could pick up some material at a reasonable price. Sewing new curtains would give me something to do in the cold, lonely evenings, especially as they'd have to be sewn by hand – I had no sewing machine.

A kettle was a must, as were a couple of mugs. I'd check out the rest of the china in the morning, but I wouldn't need much.

I glanced at the light – a bare bulb swinging from some very dodgy looking wiring. I couldn't do much about the wiring, I guessed all the wiring in the building had to pass health and safety checks so it was probably safe, but the bulb was weak and, without some sort of shade, cast a stark, uncompromising light across the room. I added light bulbs to the list and decided I could run to a lampshade – as long as it was cheap.

Canned vegetables, fruit and soup were also added as well as some cleaning materials. I'd go shopping in the morning and spend the rest of the day cleaning the flat – note that I'd stopped thinking of it as an apartment already – and making it a place fit to live in. If I could pick up some scraps of material in bright colours then I could make some scatter rugs out of scraps and that might help liven the place up a bit.

It was just as well that I hadn't got into my jimjams because around 8.15 there was a knock at the door. I unlocked the door but left the chain on.

The couple who stood on my doorstep didn't *look* too suspicious, but I wasn't taking any chances and continued to peer through the gap.

"Hi." The guy, who was long-haired, tall and not at all bad looking, held out a hand. "We're your neighbours."

I poked my hand through the gap and shook his hand. The short blonde girl with him put her hand out as well. The difference was *her* hand was holding a bottle of wine. I immediately took the chain off and threw the door open.

"Come in," I said. My mother would have told me not to invite strangers into my home but, after all, strangers are only friends you haven't met yet, aren't they? And if strangers were giving you alcohol then they must be friends, right?

"Sorry," I said, hurrying ahead of them and moving my outdoor clothes and cases, "I've only just got here."

"Yeah, we know, I'm Nathan, by the way, but everyone calls me Nat."

"Hi, Nat."

"And I'm Cindy," his blonde-haired companion said.

I smiled at her.

"And I live *that* side of you," Nat said, pointing to one wall, "and Cindy lives on *that* side." He pointed to the opposite wall.

"Oh, I thought you were a couple."

Cindy laughed. "No," Nat said, "Just very good friends." He smiled.

The sofa cleared I beckoned them to sit down. "Well, it's nice to meet you both." I nodded at the bottle. "I'll get some glasses for that."

I sorted three reasonable looking glasses from the half dozen or so in the cupboard and carried them back to my guests.

"I'm Laura, by the way."

"And you're an Aussie," Cindy exclaimed.

I laughed and shook my head. I really couldn't understand how people could mistake my soft Norfolk accent for the rather harsher Australian accent, but I supposed that was probably true of Americans and Canadians – I knew that back in England we commonly mistook them for one another.

"I'm from England," I explained, gratefully noting that Nathan had come equipped with a corkscrew – I wasn't sure whether I owned one.

"And you ended up her because –." Nathan expertly opened the bottle and poured a glass of wine and handed it to me. "Sorry, you don't have to answer that. It's nothing to do with me."

"No, you're okay. I'm here in America because I fell in love, and I'm here in this particular apartment because the guy I thought I was going to spend the rest of my life with wasn't what I thought he was."

"Men!" Cindy said, "You can't trust them, can you?"

"Hey, don't mind me." Nat feigned a hurt expression.

"Oh, sorry, present company excepted." Cindy laughed and she and Nat clinked glasses and then held them out to me.

"Welcome to the crazy place," Nat said, and we *all* clinked glasses.

"Thanks," I said. "So what's it like living here."

Cindy and Nat exchanged glances.

"Like Nat said, it can be crazy," Cindy told me, "but on the other hand it's often very calm and peaceful."

"Well, it is now that Russ has left."

"Russ?" I asked.

"Your predecessor." Nat told me. "The guy who lived here before you. Not that he was any trouble really, we hardly saw him, but some of his friends were a bit noisy."

"Yeah," Cindy took over. "And after he left some of them came and broke down the door."

This wasn't sounding very calm and peaceful to me.

"They didn't actually break *down* the door," Nat explained, "they just forced it open."

"Why?" I wanted to know.

Nathan shrugged. "Who knows? We think perhaps he owed someone some money or something."

"He ran out in the middle of the night, didn't he, Nat?"

Nat nodded. "That's right. I came out one morning and his door was wide open. All his stuff had gone."

"And we haven't seen him since." Cindy finished.

"But people have been here looking for him since he left?" I prompted, trying to keep the concern from my voice.

"Yes. But only the once and that was the day after he'd gone. I'm sure they won't be back."

Cindy, obviously realising that Nat was trying to reassure me, took up the gauntlet.

"That's right," she nodded, "after all, they know that he's not here now, don't they?"

Yes, sure, but I couldn't help wondering if there was anyone *else* who might be looking for my predecessor. And if the people looking for him hadn't found him then would they come back for another look?

"Anyway," Nat said, "Any problems, just hammer on the wall. The walls are pretty thick though," he grinned. "Just as well really, you wouldn't want to hear everything your neighbours got up to, would you?"

No, I thought, and I wouldn't mind betting that you get up to quite a lot, young fella-me-lad. You've got the bluest eyes that I've ever seen and a smile that would melt the snow from the Himalayas.

Nat and Cindy seemed like nice people and I thought that if they were typical of the people in the building then living here wasn't going to be too bad.

It had been a long day and, much as I enjoyed talking to my new friends, I was quite relieved when they left about an hour later.

This time I did dig out my pyjamas *and* my hot water bottle. It still wasn't a pleasant experience getting in between the cold sheets but I was barely awake long enough to notice.

CHAPTER TWO

I felt refreshed when I woke next morning. I'd slept well, only waking a couple of times to find the comforter was slipping away from me and my body was exposed to the cold air. And once when I needed to pee. I discovered, unsurprisingly, my new home was even colder at two in the morning than it had been at 8.30 the previous evening. I also found that the light shining in through the window from the all night diner was enough for me to see to make my way across to the loo. I glanced out of the window as I passed and noticed it was still snowing, the snow piling up on the roofs of cars left outside the bars. In the melancholy, early-morning hours the sight just reminded me how very far I was from home.

I thought about making some toast when I got up the next morning but couldn't find a toaster and didn't know if I'd have fancied using it anyway. I made a note on my shopping list that I needed a toaster and meanwhile I settled for a currant bun. I was a great believer in a good breakfast; my mother had always told me that it was the most important meal of the day. *My* idea of a good breakfast was a couple of doughnuts, which would have horrified my mother, but then this was America, wasn't it? However, not having any doughnuts to hand, the bun had to do.

Breakfast over, I dumped the plate that I'd used in the sink, fumbled through the suitcase for my sponge bag, a towel and some clean underwear and headed for the shower room. There was no heating in here so I'd left the door open all night and the heating on in the main room. Now I turned on the shower and tested the water. At least it was hot. I left the door open to the living area, stripped off my jimjams, shivered and dived under the shower.

Standing under the running water I was in absolute heaven. I could feel the heat penetrating through to my bones. Ah, this was bliss; I could happily stay in here all day. I stood and let the shower warm me and thought about home.

Home for me was a little village in Norfolk, England. I doubted whether anyone else from our village had ever ventured outside Europe, yet alone cross the Atlantic. I imagined that all the old dears in the WI must torment my mother for news of me. It probably seemed to them as if Alaska was situated on a far-flung planet somewhere in a far away universe.

Sometimes that's how it felt to me, too. At that moment I would have given anything to be standing in the big bathroom in my parents' house, towelling my hair dry with one of their soft, fluffy towels, not having to worry about the cold because I'd know that anywhere I went in my parents' house would be warm.

Tears of self-pity pricked my eyes and I brushed them away angrily. It was my fault I'd ended up here; if I'd listened to my parents I *would* still be in the bathroom at home. Well, no, it was probably about five thirty in the afternoon there now and actually if I was still at home I'd be sitting down about now to one of Mum's dinners.

My stomach rumbled.

"Shut up," I muttered, looking down at the offending part of my body. "You've had your breakfast. What more do you want?"

It remained quiet.

I dressed quickly, putting on the clean underwear and then the remainder of the clothes I'd discarded the night before. If I'd got to pay for every wash load that I did then I'd need to preserve clothes as much as I could.

I thought about unpacking my luggage but decided to wait until I'd returned from my shopping trip and cleaned all the drawers and cupboards before I started putting away my belongings.

I wrapped myself up warm and glanced out of the window. It had stopped snowing but it lay thick underfoot and the fact that the sky was clear with no sign of clouds meant that the temperature was going to have plummeted even further.

Still, this had to be done. I stuffed my gloved hands in my pocket and headed downtown.

Been here before, I thought, as I meandered through the stalls at the flea-market. When I first came over to join Glen he gave me *carte blanche* to choose all the soft furnishings and linens we'd need for our new apartment. He had to really; I was paying for them. "A little cash flow problem, babe," he'd told me, "I'll pay you back in a few days." I should have sensed a problem in the making then, but I was too blinded by love to see.

Three hours later I was back in the flat, shopping bags spread around on every possible surface. I switched on my new, yellow kettle that I'd filled with water and while it was heating I unpacked the rest of the stuff.

The toaster was yellow too, as was the background in the fabric I'd bought for the small kitchen window. I thought I'd do the tiny kitchen out in yellow and orange, while I could cheer up the living area with bright greens and blues.

I felt quite cheerful as I drank my coffee. I was lucky to be able to have vision when it came to decorating and I could see how the flat would look once I'd finished. A damn sight better than it did now!

For the rest of the day I scrubbed and cleaned and polished. By the time that I fell into bed that night I was exhausted but everything was put away in appropriate places and the faces of my parents smiled at me from the picture frame on my bedside cabinet.

Quite a bit of mail came for my predecessor during my first few weeks in the flat. A lot of it was obviously circulars and I threw these in the bin, but some looked like bills and others like personal letters and I didn't know what to do with them. I decided that I'd check with Con sometime and see if he had a forwarding address for the guy. Meanwhile I stacked the mail that came for Russ Bracken on a shelf in the kitchen - a kitchen that was now looking bright and cheery with its new curtains and paintwork.

There were also fresh curtains in the living room and a matching rug and throw over the sofa. I'd toyed with the idea of pulling up the carpet itself and perhaps sanding the floorboards but I didn't know what the boards were like and, for the moment, decided not to take a chance. Instead I'd bought a cheap rug which replaced the old, stained one and still covered the burn holes in the carpet.

It was on a Sunday that the girl first appeared at my door. I'd been in the flat for 17 days. My visitor was clutching a baby - a little boy, I guessed, seeing as he was dressed head to toe in powder blue. Judging by his size the baby couldn't be more than a few weeks old,

The girl looked appalled when I opened the door. She looked at me, her mouth dropped open and she burst into tears.

I asked her what was wrong, but she seemed to be having difficulty forming coherent words. Somewhere amongst the babble that was coming from her mouth I though I discerned the word "Russ".

I couldn't leave her bawling on the doorstep so I invited her in. Still crying, she entered the flat and collapsed on the sofa. I handed her a box of tissues and she wiped her eyes with her free hand, the other one clutching the baby tightly.

I sat beside her and waited for her to compose herself so that she could tell me what all the fuss was about.

Eventually she calmed down. In the meantime I'd stood up again and put the kettle on and got a couple of mugs out.

It soon became clear that she thought I was cohabiting with her boyfriend – Russ, of course. The girl told me that her name was Sara and that Russ was the father of her baby. Sara was expecting Russ to make his child legitimate.

I put her clear on the facts; that I'd never met Russ, but that he had vacated the flat and I was now the tenant. She seemed relieved, confused and upset by my explanation.

"We're supposed to be getting married," She sniffled as I handed her a coffee, which she took with her free hand – her other hand being wrapped round the baby still. "He promised."

"Why didn't he marry you as soon as you knew you were pregnant?" I asked, thinking that this Russ sounded like a complete waste of space. "And why have you left it this long to come round and see what was happening?"

"He offered," she sniffed, "but I didn't want to spend the rest of my life wondering if he'd only married me because I was pregnant. I told him to ask me again once the baby was born."

"And did he?"

"Yes. He was with me all through the birth and as soon as Tommy" she looked down at her baby with adoring eyes, "was born, he said '*now* will you marry me?'" She returned her gaze to me. "And, of course, I said 'yes'. We've booked the church and everything." The enormity of her situation seemed to hit her then and she gave in to a fresh flood of weeping.

"That still doesn't explain why you've left it this long to come round," I said, moving the box of tissues closer.

"He was away," she said, her voice breaking. "He went two days after Tommy was born and was supposed to be coming back yesterday."

"So have you heard from him while he's been away?" I asked.

She shook her head. "No," and dissolved into another fit of weeping.

"Is that usual?" I asked. Surely if these two were engaged and planning a wedding she would have been on the 'phone to him every five minutes.

She shook her head, unable to speak for the sobs.

I left her and went to the kitchen to collect the personal correspondence that had been delivered for Russ.

"These came for Russ," I said, placing them on the arm of the sofa. "I didn't know what to do with them and as it seems as if you're the closest thing I can come up with to a next of kin, I'm passing the buck to you."

Sara stuffed tissues in her pocket, sniffed, and picked up the letters. She looked from the envelopes to back and me again.

"Do you think I should open them?" she asked in a wobbly voice. "It might give us a clue as to where Russ is."

Now I'm just like the next person, I'd been *dying* to open the letters since they arrived but I was scared that Russ might turn up one day to claim them so I'd been very good and resisted. Sara was virtually Russ' next of kin, right? Therefore, it stood to reason that she should open them, and best that I encourage her to open them now while she was with me rather than later when she might be on her own. You didn't know, did you? There might be bad news in them and she ought to have someone with her just in case.

I nodded, trying not to appear too eager. "I think so," I said.

There were seven or eight envelopes – hell, I knew that there were exactly eight. The first one was a disappointment; although the envelope was hand-written, the content was simply a flyer for a local theatre. The second one appeared to be from a guy called James, a friend of Russ's. Sara said Russ often talked about James; he and James occasionally went on hunting trips together. My opinion of Russ sunk a bit lower. I know that I was in Alaska, which is one of the hunting capitals of the world, but I came from England. I'd protested along with other animal rights campaigners against such things as fox hunting and I still couldn't understand how anyone could get pleasure from slaughtering another living creature.

The letter didn't give any clues as to Russ' whereabouts; it was just general keep-in-touch chat. "He says that he hopes to see Russ and his new family later in the year."

Uh-oh, here came the tears again. "So Russ must have written him about me and Tommy," she said, her voice catching in her throat. Another handful of tissues was dragged from the box.

"Didn't Russ invite James to the wedding?" I asked.

"No," Sara sniffed. "It was going to be a very small wedding, just my family and a couple of really close friends."

The third and fourth envelope held more flyers, a local diner and Chinese restaurant. Didn't these people have mailing lists and computers, I wondered? Shouldn't these envelopes by typed, not hand-written, thereby avoiding the recipient supposing the envelope was going to contain something interesting.

The next envelope was a final reminder for his cell 'phone contract and the following one told him he'd won a million dollar prize in a lottery.

Definitely a scam, we decided and threw that one in the bin. The one concerning his cell 'phone I put to one side; I'd write and advise the company that Russ no longer lived here. I didn't want them sending in the bailiffs.

The remaining two envelopes appeared to be addressed in the same handwriting.

Sara slit one open, pulled out the sheets of paper and sat reading.

"Oh. My. God."

"What? What is it?" Didn't this girl know how frustrating it was for me to sit by just waiting? Anyone with a smidgen of empathy would have given me some of the letters to open – after all, it was *my* sofa she was sitting on and *my* mug she was drinking from and *my* coffee that she was drinking. Not to mention it was my box of tissues that she was working her way through at a rate of knots.

Instead I was left holding the baby. She'd given me little Tommy when I'd made the mistake of sitting back down next to her after bringing the mail through and I had to admit he had the cutest little button nose and an adorable smile but - I sniffed - an appalling smell.

"Er, I think that Tommy might need changing" I offered.

No response. Sara simply continued to gaze at the letter.

"Sara? *Sara!"*

Slowly she moved her attention from the letter to me. "He was married," she wailed. "Russ was *married.*" The look on her face was one of total disbelief.

I forgot about Tommy momentarily, I was so concerned for Sara. She'd gone very pale and I thought she might pass out.

Quickly, I grabbed her head with my spare hand that wasn't holding the baby, and thrust it down between her knees. She struggled. "Oi! Let go!"

"I was just …" What I was just trying to do hung in the air.

"I'm all right," she protested, pushing my arm away. "It was just a shock."

"I take it you didn't know that he was married?"

Doh. Dumb question.

"Of course I didn't. We-ell ,,,,"

"Yes?" I prompted.

"I knew that he *was* married. When we met. He told me he and his wife had been living apart for ages and he more or less said that the divorce was going through. Obviously when he asked me to marry him I assumed it *had* gone through. The way she writes though, I don't think that *she* knows." Sara held out the letter to me and I took it from her.

The letter wasn't particularly *loving*; it was more of a friend writing than a spouse. In fact, if she hadn't signed it "your loving wife" I would have thought that it *was* from a friend.

Sara, meanwhile, had slit open the other envelope and was busily reading the letter it had contained. "Oh, hang on," she said, "this is from her, too, and this one refers to a divorce. She says that she wishes him well for the future and hopes that they will continue to be friends after the divorce becomes final." Sara turned her attention to me. "You'd think that he would have mentioned it to me, wouldn't you?"

You would indeed, but then this was Russ we were talking about and I was beginning to realise that he wasn't a man who behaved as one would expect.

"I guess that he thought that you'd got enough on your plate without worrying about his marital status."

Why was I making excuses for the rat? I supposed that it was because I already liked Sara. I didn't want her to be any more hurt than necessary. "Talking of which," I continued, holding Tommy out towards her, "I think this young man needs some attention."

"Oh, sure." Sara put the letter down and rifled through the large bag it contained. She pulled some things from it, stood up and took Tommy in her arms. She stood looking round. "Oh, I was going to change him in the restroom but it isn't big enough, is it?"

There was barely room to stand in the shower room. When I cleaned my teeth this morning I'd banged my elbow against the side of the shower cubicle.

"In here," I told her, gesturing towards the floor.

"Oh," she looked doubtful; "I don't really like …." Her voice trailed off.

"There isn't anywhere else," I said. "Just go ahead. I'll put the kettle on again."

I collected the mugs and went through to the kitchen where I proceeded to wash up and make us each a fresh coffee. I didn't really want to be in the same room as a baby who was having his soiled nappy changed, however cute a nose he'd got.

"What did Russ actually do for a living?" I called out.

"He was some sort of salesman, so he was away travelling a lot of the time." Sara appeared at the kitchen door with Tommy in her arms.

16

Quick job, but then I supposed if you were changing nappies numerous time every day then you got quite efficient at it.

"Like I said," Sara continued, "that's why I hadn't been round sooner. I thought he was away working, but I have to admit that I was worried that I didn't hear from him. Normally he 'phones me or emails me on my Dad's pc, depending on whether or not Russ has access to email. I tried calling him but I couldn't get through on his cell 'phone. And there's been no reply to my emails. I was getting *really* worried …." Her voice trailed off.

I carried the coffee back into the living room. "So how long has it been since you saw him?"

Sara shrugged. "Nearly three weeks, I guess."

Three weeks. I'd looked at the apartment a fortnight ago. Surely Con would have left the apartment for longer than a week before re-letting it. Unless he *knew* the occupier wasn't coming back?

"Did Russ come back here?" I asked, "After Tommy was born."

Sara picked up her coffee. "No, he went on the road straight from my house. He always travelled light and, anyway, had bought stuff with him so that he was ready to head off as soon as Tommy made an appearance."

Curious, I thought. I had a few questions that I needed to ask Con.

CHAPTER THREE

I didn't like Con's secretary, and she didn't like me. Come to that I wasn't that fond of Con. Just because he was some kind of relative didn't mean I had to like him, did it? I think the secretary, who'd obviously got the hots for Con (there was no accounting for taste), saw me as some kind of threat, just because I *was* related. So when I rang and she told me that Con was out of the office showing someone round a property and that she'd get him to ring me when he returned I wondered if she'd actually pass on the message. I decided I'd give it an hour before I rang and reminded her. An hour should be long enough for Con to show someone round the Taj Mahal. Con didn't allow prospective clients to linger long in case they spotted something that they may not like. Instead he hurried them round a house or apartment and practically shoved a pen in their hand before they were out of the door, so keen was he for them to sign a contract.

I hadn't signed a contract. Con said that as we were related we could take it on trust. I knew that meant that I could be turned out anytime, but it also meant that I could *leave* at any time and not be held liable for any outstanding rent. I considered the arrangement suited both of us.

Now I was trying to get in touch with Con to see if *he* had any idea where Russ was.

"The office will be closed," Sara had protested, "It's Sunday."

I pointed out that Russ always opened on Sunday, but closed on Wednesdays instead. "People tend to want to look at property at the weekend," I explained, "when they're not at work."

I put the 'phone down. "Not there," I said to Sara. "I'll try again later."

"Okay." Sara seemed to be cheering up a bit now that we were actually doing something constructive. Maybe it just helped having someone else on her side.

"Did Russ have an office that he worked from?" I asked Sara.

"Oh yes, but I never went there, I don't even know where it is, somewhere between fifth and sixth avenue, I think he said, but I can't be sure."

"So he would probably have a computer there, and email? Do you think the office would know where he is?"

She shook her head. "No. I have their number and I called them last week. They told me that as far as they knew Russ was on the road somewhere. They'd expected him to call in but so far he hadn't. In fact they were worried themselves and were planning on calling some of the firms Russ was supposed to be visiting to see if he'd carried out the calls he was supposed to have done. They promised me they'd let me know if he did call in or if they heard anything."

I was overwhelmed again by the cut-off feeling somebody who's been used to having internet access gets when they no longer have that life-line. When I got over to Alaska and found that Glen didn't have a computer I'd obviously planned on getting one. Luckily I hadn't got round to it, I knew now that Glen would only have flogged it if I had. These days I used the computer at the local library to email friends and family in the UK, or the one at work, although the one at work was monitored occasionally, so I used it sparingly. There weren't actually any strict rules that we *couldn't* use the office email for personal use, but I didn't want them to get the idea that was all I did while I was at my place of work so I only used it to send a couple of emails every day. Just keeping in touch with my family. I missed having that link to the outside world when I was at home though.

"Presumably you've left messages on his cell 'phone?" I asked.

"Yeah. Text and voice mail."

"And he hasn't got back to you?"

"Not since the first week." She'd already told me that they'd spoken every day the first week he'd been away. Just a few minutes a day. "He liked to touch base," she said fondly. Then the calls had stopped.

"I don't know what to do," she wailed. Tommy joined in and the apartment was suddenly filled with the sound of misery.

I didn't know what to do either. And why was I feeling responsible for this girl? A girl that up until a few hours ago I had no idea even *existed!*

I supposed that it must be something to do with my occupying Russ' flat. But I wasn't personally responsible for turning him out of his home, was I? Okay, so it was opportune for me that he'd left when he did, but I'd have found another flat – sorry, *apartment* if he'd still been living in this one.

Suddenly both mother and baby fell silent; a real mother and baby connection. Sara pulled out some more tissues and Tommy's eyes followed her movements.

Sighing, I went and put the kettle on - *again*. This time I got out a packet of cookies as well. Sara had been here through lunchtime and it was now mid-afternoon, but my cupboards didn't stock enough for a meal for two, so the cookies were aimed at holding off starvation for a while. Seemed to me that Tommy was the only one who was being fed to capacity round here. Sara had unself-consciously already breast fed him twice.

"So Sara," I said, putting yet another mug of coffee on the floor beside her and offering her the plate of cookies, "you're living with your parents, are you?"

"Yes. They've been great." She took a couple of the biscuits and smiled. When she smiled, Sara looked about 16, but I guessed that she was several years older than that. "They were pretty upset at first about the baby but once they got used to the idea they rolled with it. Jeez, Laura, they're going to be devastated. All that money they've paid out."

I could see that the tissues were in for another bashing. It was a wonder that there were any left. Then what she'd said began to dawn on me. "Haven't you told them about Russ disappearing?" I asked when the sobs appeared to be subsiding.

Sara shook her head. "I didn't want to worry them unless it was absolutely necessary. They've just assumed that we've been in constant touch. It looks like I'm going to have to tell them now though."

My cell 'phone rang then and I could tell from the read-out that it was my Mum.

"Crap!" I muttered.

"Problems?"

Now here's the thing. I hadn't told Mum I was no longer living with Glen. Hadn't wanted to admit what a sod he had turned out to be. It would be humiliating to admit that they'd been right and I'd been wrong. I'd told Mum that we'd moved and given her my current address, but she thought that I was living here with Glen. I'd made the apartment sound pretty grand compared to what it actually was, implying that the living room and kitchen were large, the bedroom had an en-suite; oh, and that the 'phone line was down rather than admit that I couldn't afford to have one connected, which was why she was ringing me on my cell. I hated talking to her though – no, that was wrong, I *loved* talking to her but I hated lying to her.

I grimaced in response to Sara's question and pressed the green button on the 'phone.

"Hi, Mum."

"Hello, darling. How's things?"

"Fine. You know, same ole, same ole."

"Well, Dad and I are just off to bed but we hadn't heard from you for a while so thought we'd just give you a quick ring. I take it that you haven't got that computer yet?"

"No, Mum. Still haven't decided on what I want." I didn't know how long I was going to get away with this. I'd been over here for six months and Mum was dying for me to get my own pc so that she and I could chat online. I kept telling her that I was happy enough on the 'phone, her voice was less distorted than it might be online, and hearing her voice made her seem closer somehow. Sooner or later she was going to get suspicious.

"Well, darling, I've got a surprise for you."

"Oh?"

"Dad and I are coming over for Christmas."

"What? Here?" *Oh, my God, how was I going to get out of this one?*

"Of course there, darling. I know you won't want to come home this Christmas, you'll want to spend it with Glen in your new home, but I can't bear to be this far apart from you at such a special time of year. Don't worry, I know you haven't got a spare room, so Dad and I are booking into a hotel."

My mind was working overtime. How could I prevent them coming over? Maybe if I offered to arrange their accommodation then I could tell them all the hotels were fully booked. After all, it was Christmas we were talking about.

"I could sort that out for you, mum. I could ask around and see where the best hotel is, that sort of thing."

"No need," Mum said cheerily, "It's all arranged. We've booked online. Had a look at a map of the town and found a hotel just round the corner from you, so it won't be too far to walk home in the evening if Dad's had a few."

Damn and bugger! What the hell was I going to do now? "Oh, great, Mum," I said, trying to keep the despair from my voice.

"Oh well, I expect you're busy." I don't think I'd succeeded; *Mum* sounded miserable now. I think she must have picked up that I wasn't over-the-moon-full–to-the-brim-with-happiness that they were coming over. "I'll let you go. Bye, bye, darling."

The connection was broken and I burst into tears. Now I'd upset Mum and that was the last thing that I wanted to do.

"Hey, what's up?" Sara had stood up and had her free arm round me. This was an abrupt role-swap, wasn't it?

I flopped down on the sofa and poured out the whole sorry story. By the time I finished we were both clutching tissues and blubbing, until I caught Sara's eye and somehow the tears turned to giggles and from there it was a small step to out and out laughter. The fact that the laughter had a slightly hysterical edge to it simply reflected our states of mind, I guess.

In the end we were both holding our sides. "I don't know why I'm l-l-laughing," I stuttered, "I'm so unhappy."

Somehow that set us off into fresh gales of mirth. Tommy joined in, his little gurgles just adding to the cacophony of sound.

Eventually emotions subsided. Sara, still clutching Tommy with her left arm, lifted her free hand and brushed her long, black hair back from her face.

"Why don't you just tell your Mum and Dad?" she asked.

"Oh, I couldn't, Sara. You don't know what they were like when I told them I was emigrating. Not only were they shattered that I was going to be living so far away, they were appalled that I was going to be living with Glen. They didn't like him, you see. They tried to put me off him but I thought it was just because they didn't want me leaving – I'm an only child and I thought they just saw themselves fading into a lonely old age. Then they gave me a lot of money when I left. Turns out they'd been saving it for my wedding but thought that if I was starting a new life in a new country it would be more use to me now." I helped myself to the last tissue in the box. "That's pretty much gone now. How could I admit that to them?"

Sara shrugged. "You'd be surprised. I didn't think that I was going to be able to tell my parents I was pregnant." She smiled. "But it's not the kind of thing that you can keep a secret for too long, is it? Eventually I had to tell them. I can't say they didn't rant and rave a bit at first, but they met Russ and they liked him, particularly when he told them that he'd asked me to marry him and that I was the one who had refused. Now they've got a grandson they adore," she looked down at Tommy who had finally dropped off to sleep, "and they've still got me and they were expecting to have a son-in-law as well." The thought of the missing Russ started the tears flowing again. She reached for a tissue and found the box empty. "Jeez, Laura, you've used all the tissues."

That started us off giggling again. Eventually, Sara put Tommy in my bed and tucked him in before building a barrier of pillows, towels and coats down one side.

"He doesn't normally move around much in his sleep, but I'll keep an eye on him."

I picked my cell 'phone up. "Gonna ring my Mum," I said. "I'm not going to tell her the truth, I'm not feeling strong enough for that, but at least I'll reassure her that I really want them to come over."

"Didn't you say that they were just going to bed?"

"Crap! Yes. That was half an hour ago. They'll be asleep by now."
I put the 'phone down.

I suspected that Mum wouldn't be asleep. She'd probably be lying awake worrying that her only child was growing away from her. I picked the 'phone up. On the other hand Dad *would* be asleep. He'd probably been asleep by the time that Mum crawled into bed after talking to me, so I'd wake him up if I called. I put the 'phone down again.

"I'll ring them in the morning. Meanwhile," I stood up and put on my coat, "I'll nip out and get us a bottle of red. Is red okay with you or would you prefer white? Or," I added as an afterthought, "Would you prefer a beer?" Then I looked at the baby. "Or perhaps a soft drink?"

"Red's good. Mustn't have much though," she nodded towards the bed. "Not while I'm breast-feeding." Sara picked up her purse and took some bills from it. She handed them to me. "Pick up some food while you're out. I know that I've kept you from yours today."

I tried to brush the money aside but Sara insisted I take it. "I know you've not got a lot and here I've been drinking all your coffee. Just get some cold cuts or something we can nibble. I'd go myself but there's Tommy."

She looked over at the bed again where Tommy was making little snuffling noises in his sleep. God, but he was adorable.

"Okay. See you in a bit." I let myself out of the apartment, glad that my mother couldn't see me now, leaving someone that I hadn't even known this morning alone in the flat. Mum would say I was foolish but, if the worst came to the worst, what could I lose? It's not as though the flat was filled with valuables. The most valuable things that I owned were on my finger, the diamond and amethyst ring that my parents had bought me for my 18th birthday two years ago and the antique ruby and pearl ring that had been my grandmother's.

So was I going to tell Mum and Dad the truth, I wondered as I jogged along the pavement? I tended to jog a lot these days; it helped keep me warm when I was in sub-zero temperatures.

I knew that they would have to know the facts when they came over; they would be glaring them in the face. Mum and Dad expected to spend time with us in the apartment they thought that I was sharing with Glen. An apartment that I'd made sound grander than it actually was, so even more of a contrast to my present home. When they found out the truth would they think that they'd wasted all that money coming over?

On the other hand they'd already booked their hotel and, presumably, paid a deposit and from what Mum was saying they'd already booked and paid for the 'plane tickets. So they'd lose all that money if they cancelled – which they might do if I told them the truth now.

Or would they still want to come? And if they didn't come would that be such a bad thing? I didn't really want them to see the hovel I was living in. Okay, it wasn't that bad, but I don't think that they ever envisaged their one and only offspring living in what was virtually a one-roomed flat.

Bugger! What should I do? I suppose that I could leave it until they arrived and say that Glen and I had only split up a couple of days before, then it wouldn't seem so bad that I hadn't told them. On the other hand Mum was sure to want to get in touch with Con while she was here, and he'd tell her that I'd been living in the flat, *alone,* for over two months. Besides, she knew that because she had the address and when she saw the flat she'd know there really wasn't room enough for two people. Sod it. I'd have to tell them soon. At least they would have got over most of their hurt and disappointment by the time I finally saw them.

Oh, but if I told them the truth then they might decide not to come over for Christmas. My mind was going round and round in circles.

Never mind that they'd be disappointed in me and I'd have to admit to where I was living, I suddenly realised how very much I was looking forward to their visit. An hour ago I hadn't known that they *were* visiting, but now the idea of *not* seeing them at Christmas was almost unbearable.

I finally faced up to the fact. I was desperately homesick.

CHAPTER FOUR

Con rang the next morning. I'd forgotten all about him for the rest of Sara's visit; *her* concerns pushed aside by my own. However, when she'd left at about 11.30 she reminded me. Actually we were both slightly the worse for wear by then, having consumed two bottles of wine (she'd sent me out for another one later in the evening – she paid, so that was okay. Oh, and she said she'd bottle-feed Tommy for the next couple of feeds. If I thought this was a bit irresponsible I kept my thoughts to myself, I'd just been happy to have a drinking pal.)

I knew that Con's office would be closed by then, but I guessed correctly that there would be an answer-phone so I rang anyway. "It's Laura, Laura Evans," I said. "Could you call me, please, Con?" I recited my number and cut the connection.

Whether Con had picked up the message himself or his secretary had eventually passed my message on I didn't know, but it was early when he called.

"You rang?" Con's voice was quite sexy if you liked that sort of thing, deep and husky. If you'd never seen him you'd conjure up a picture of a tall, drop-dead gorgeous hunk with film-star looks. I *had* seen him though, and I knew he resembled a slug more than he resembled Brad Pitt.

"Ah, yes, Con. I wanted to speak to you about the guy who lived in the flat before me-"

"You are *not* living in a flat," Con interrupted me, "Over here it's called an apartment."

I was tempted to point out that the word "apartment" conjured up a picture of something rather grander than this crummy joint, but I bit my tongue. There really wasn't a lot of point in antagonising him.

I put on my best apologising voice. "Sorry, Con, of course it's an apartment. It's just with me being English and all that the word 'flat' feels more comfortable."

I heard him make a "tsk" sound but I carried on, "anyway, Con, do you know anything about the guy?"

"Why? That apartment was cleaned thoroughly before it was re-let. There was nothing left over from a previous tenant." Con's voice was raising several tones. He was on the defensive. Did he have so many complaints about properties he let out that he assumed every one who called was going to complain?

Probably.

"Con, there's nothing wrong with the fl – apartment, it's fine." If you like living in a hovel, I added to myself. "It's just that people are looking for the guy. His name's Russ, by the way, Russ Brecken, or Breacken, or something."

"Russ Bracken," Con said. "*Who's* looking for him?"

"His girl-friend for one. She's had his baby and they're supposed to be getting married soon. And now she doesn't know where he is. And there were some other people round here apparently. You must know about them, they broke down the door."

"The door was fixed." Con said. "There's nothing wrong with the door."

I was losing patience. "I didn't say there was, Con. All I'm asking is do you have any idea where this Russ Bracken is now?"

"Of course I don't. I'm not my tenants' keeper – not when they're no longer a tenant anyway."

"You did let out the flat – sorry, *apartment* - pretty soon after he left though. You must have known that he wasn't coming back. It's not normal to re-let so soon, surely?"

"The fact that the bastard had taken all his clothes and owed me a month's rent was a good indication that he wasn't coming back. Besides, I needed to recoup some of that lost revenue."

Oh, heaven forbid that you should miss out on any money, Con.

"So you're saying you've no idea where Russ is then? You don't know of any leads we could follow?"

"No, I don't. What's it got to do with you anyway? I thought you'd got enough problems of your own without taking on anybody else's."

Damn, I forgot. I hadn't intended to pour my heart out to Con – he wasn't the kindly-uncle type, but it had been a really bad day when I'd looked at the flat, and I'd found myself bawling my eyes out in the car on the way back to the real estate office. The flat had looked better than it did on the day I moved in, sure, but it was still nothing like the home I thought I'd be living in. It had just been disappointment following disappointment since I came to Alaska and, much as I loved the country and the people, I felt let down by life in general.

I'd blurted all this out to Con and I didn't really think he'd been listening, but he'd obviously taken it in.

"It's called empathy, Con," I said now. "Feeling someone else's hurt and wanting to do something about it. Still, I don't suppose you'd

26

recognise empathy if it jumped up and hit you in the face, would you?" I clicked the 'phone off.

Damn. Now I'd been rude to him. He'd probably come round and throw me out of the flat, and, dump though it was, I hadn't anywhere else to go.

I flopped on to the sofa and looked round the room. Actually, it wasn't *that* bad. The building's structure seemed sound, the walls thick, the glass in the windows intact, and now I'd tarted it up a bit the room looked halfway respectable. The kitchen and shower-room were tiny, sure, but the main living area was pretty spacious and seemed the more so because I had so few belongings with which to fill it.

The carpet still looked grimy and took the tone down a notch or two but there wasn't much I could do about that. I might make a few more scatter rugs, cheer it up a bit more.

I gave myself a mental shake. I'd got to stop thinking that I'd sunk to the bottom of the pond. Maybe I had, but I was starting to claw my way up again. I had a good job that I enjoyed and I earned enough to be able to afford a small treat every week – this usually took the form of alcohol - and I was also putting a teeny-weeny bit of money in the bank for what I knew - but didn't admit to myself - was my "going home fund". Plus I had good neighbours (Cindy, Nat and I had spent a bit of time together since I'd been living in the flat and they were great company) and now a new "best mate" in Sara. The fact that Sara had problems of her own would help me take my mind off my own worries.

Feeling a little more cheerful I dialled Mum's number. It would be mid afternoon back home now and she'd probably been worrying all day. I really should have called her before I went to bed last night; I'd probably have caught her before she left for work.

"Hello, darling," she sounded cautious.

"Hi, Mum. Look, Mum, I just wanted to tell you how thrilled I am that you're coming over for Christmas."

"You are?" I was pleased to hear her voice sounded happier.

"Of course I am, Mum. I can't wait."

"Oh, that's all right then. I was a little worried yesterday that we'd overstepped the mark by inviting ourselves over."

"Oh, Mum, don't be daft. You're my parents. How *could* you overstep the mark? Sorry if I sounded a bit off yesterday, I'd got a friend here and she was upset about something."

"Well, as long as you're happy?"

"Course I am. Can't wait. Gotta go now or I'll be late for work."

"Bye then, darling."

I cut the connection and it was with a new lightness of step that I set off for work that morning. Actually, my steps weren't literally light at all; my feet were weighed down as they were every morning by the heavy boots that I wore. Ribbed rubber soles kept me from slipping around on the ice. Luckily, the girls in the office had warned me about the winter and I'd kitted myself out with appropriate outerwear before the snows started.

I'd wondered, when I first arrived, how they managed to start the vehicles in the sub-zero temperatures and had been told tales of people fitting electric thermal pads on to engines and batteries and fitting anti-freeze jackets around various engine components. Humans, like animals, adapted to their conditions.

The roads in the towns and cities were kept pretty clear, but I wondered how people in outlying areas got on. I knew that many of them simply holed up for the winter and didn't venture out until early spring. It was a romanticised view of Alaskan life that lots of people held. They conjured up pictures of log cabins, open fires and bearskin rugs. In reality I supposed that it must get very lonely and put a strain on even the strongest of relationships. On the other hand, if that was what they were used to I guessed that they adapted and made provision for those long nights. You couldn't live like that and not have a hobby!

Glen had made it clear that we would be living in a busy town, so I'd never imagined that I might be living in a log cabin. Well, actually, I *had*. The idea of making love on a fur (*faux*, of course) rug in front of a roaring fire in a log cabin surrounded by six foot of snow appealed very strongly. I'd imagined that Glen and I might rent a cabin for a week or so in the winter, forgetting that the roads to such log cabins would be completely impassable and not knowing that Glen hadn't got two cents to rub together, despite the appearance he'd given when I met him. My imaginings – or dreams – had swiftly turned to dust.

I called Sara at lunchtime. She said that she hadn't dared breast feed little Tommy at all after all the wine she'd drunk yesterday and it seemed like this might be a good time to wean him on to the bottle full time.

We arranged to meet up at the weekend. Her Dad would pick me up in his 4x4 around ten on Saturday morning and I could spend the day with them. She offered me a bed for the night, but I'd arranged to have Sunday lunch with Nat and Cindy and I thought it best that I was back in my own bed the previous night. Besides, I had been pleasantly surprised by how comfortable my bed was and I always quite looked forward to snuggling up in my own little corner of the world. I was becoming quite proprietal about the flat. It was *my* space – well, I knew it wasn't really, it was Con's, or whoever he was an agent for, but for the time being it was mine.

I can't deny though, that the idea of a proper bath in a proper sized bathroom appealed and I thought that if I were ever invited again I'd probably take Sara up on it just so that I could enjoy their bath. Didn't want to outstay my welcome on my first visit though.

It would be nice to do something different at the weekend. The television in the flat *did* work, although the picture was a bit suspect and not easy to watch. I read a lot though, borrowing books from the library. I was in and out of the library frequently, picking up and replying to emails, so I had a big turnover of library books. Sometimes on a Friday night I'd go out for a drink – okay, *a few* drinks – with Maisie from work. This week I was finding a lot of my time was taken up with thoughts of Russ and Sara, not to mention worrying about my parents and their Christmas visit.

Christmas! Damn. I needed to buy some presents. I'd got less than two months and I must buy for my Mum and Dad if for nobody else. There goes my fund, I thought, and there wasn't a lot of dosh in that!

I wondered about taking on an evening job. I could work in one of the bars that littered the streets perhaps. It would help the fund grow and give me some extra income towards Christmas. I resolved to take a walk round one day, preferably a day when it wasn't actually snowing, and check out all the bars. I'd ask around too. Cindy and Nat might be able to help. Nat played in a band that worked a lot locally, so he might know of any bars that were hiring, and Cindy – well, Cindy was a pole dancer.

Funny, I'd always imagined that pole dancers tended to be slim and tall and beautiful. Cindy was short and a little bit on the dumpy side. However, while she wasn't beautiful she was very pretty and I could imagine that she was probably extremely popular with both punters and colleagues. She had a cheerful, outgoing personality with an almost permanent smile.

I had thought that Cindy and Nat were an item, but as I got to know them better I realised that they were just very good friends. Cindy had lived in her apartment for three years and had worked various clubs in the area. Nat, who at 19 was a year younger than Cindy, had only been in his apartment just over a year. Nat had a succession of girlfriends but nobody serious, while Cindy had been going out with Tony, her boyfriend, for more than two years.

"Doesn't he mind?" I asked her when she'd told me what she did for a living.

"Mind? Don't be silly. He loves it. The idea of other men desiring me," Cindy looked a little coy at this point, as though she still had difficulty believing that men *did* desire her, "and knowing that it's him I'll be going home with thrills him to bits. It adds something extra to our love-making" she nudged me with her elbow, "if you know what I mean.

Cindy spoke in a very high-pitched voice which, when she got excited, turned into a squeak. I thought it was fortunate that pole dancers didn't have to speak. I imagined one or two men might be turned off by her voice but then who knew, these were men I was talking about! It would probably take a lot more than the tone of a voice to turn them off.

Nat, by contrast, had a voice that spoke of the Deep South, a kind of Elvis drawl that I found attractive in men and harsh and unattractive in women. He came from Memphis, the buckle on the Bible belt. Nat's sister had married an Alaskan she'd met on the Internet and had moved up here following her marriage. Shortly after her marriage Nat's father had suffered a stroke from which he never completely recovered. Nat's parents sold the farm they had farmed for thirty years and, with Nat, had moved north and downsized their home so that they had enough to live on with just Nat's mum working part time. Nat had left home when he was 18 after a row with his mother. They had made up now though and Nat saw his parents regularly, although they lived fifty miles away, but Nat stayed on in his flat.

It was comforting to have people I felt comfortable with living either side of me, especially because I knew that I could call on either one of them if I needed to.

I needed to when I got home that night!

CHAPTER FIVE

I was feeling optimistic as I walked home from work that night. I'd decided that I wouldn't tell my parents about my break up with Glen prior to their arrival. They'd only worry. Once they were here they'd be able to see that I was coping and enjoying life and that they had nothing to worry about.

I congratulated myself on pulling myself together after the trauma of the break up with Glen and getting on with my life. I'd got a nice flat (okay, *apartment)* that had more than enough room to swing a cat in, and it was cheerful and now felt like home. And I was determined that no cheating, thieving guy was ever going to take the few possessions I'd managed to accumulate away from me; I wasn't going to be caught like that again.

I'd got friends – *good* friends; friends that I know would be there for me if I needed them. I'd found the Alaskan people really sociable. I guess when you lived in that kind of climate you had to be ready to help one another out and that made for an easy, outgoing population.

Yes, I thought, as I climbed the stairs, it was good to come home after a day in the office and know that the flat was mine.

There was no indication that there was anything wrong as I approached the flat. It wasn't until I reached the door and I realised that it wasn't actually closed, just pulled to, that I got the feeling that something wasn't quite as it should be.

I stepped back from the door, my heart thudding in my chest. I know that I'd said that there was nothing worth stealing in the flat, but I'd lied. There was the new kettle and toaster and my lovely curtains and – sod it! I stepped forward and put my hand out –

And stopped.

Supposing there was someone still in the flat? Supposing he'd got a knife – or a gun? This was, after all, America.

On the other hand, perhaps I'd not closed the door behind me this morning? I tried to remember. I'd called Mum, put my boots on, wrapped myself up warm and left. No matter how I tried, I couldn't quite see myself closing the door. On the other hand, I couldn't see myself leaving it open either. It was one of those things that you do automatically and I was *sure* I must have closed it securely when I left.

I dithered. I couldn't hear anything from inside the flat but that didn't mean anything, someone could be lying in wait for me to barge in unsuspectingly. Oh no, that didn't work, they'd know that I would suspect something because the door wasn't closed.

I took a deep breath. . .

And knocked on Nathan's door.

It could just have easily been Cindy's door I knocked on but I thought Nathan might just have the edge over Cindy if it came to a bit of the rough stuff.

"Hi, hun." Nathan was rubbing his eyes and I guessed that he'd just woken up.

"I think my flat's been broken into," I whispered. "The door's not closed."

Nat took a look at my door. "Sure you didn't just forget to close it this morning?" He, too, whispered.

"Of course I'm sure. I remember closing it and checking it was locked when I left." I lied. I didn't want Nat to think I wasn't sure.

"Hang on." Nat disappeared into his room and there was the sound of things being thrown about. He appeared again a few seconds later. "Couldn't find my shoes," he said sheepishly.

"I thought there might be someone still in there," I said, waving in the general direction of my flat.

Nat looked at me. "You think so?" He shrugged and walked towards the door, bypassed it and knocked on Cindy's door. Cindy appeared, wearing her work clothes and very little else.

"Hi, gang. What's up?"

"Laura thinks her flat might have been broken into and she's worried that the perp might still be in there."

Perp? You've been watching too many TV cop series, Nat.

Cindy was out of the door and into my flat in the blink of an eye. No hesitation, she just marched in! Nat and I followed, somewhat more cautiously.

Cindy stood just inside the doorway. "Anyone here?" she called. I was impressed; I wouldn't have *dared* do that. Perhaps the extra five inches her shoes added to her height gave her confidence.

There was no answer and Cindy walked further into the room. "Oh dear," she said.

"What? What is it?" Now I was confident that there wasn't a mad-axe-murderer lurking in the shadows of the flat I rushed in to stand beside Cindy. And gazed at the melee that used to be my home.

"Crap!"

"An understatement, my dear, I rather think." Cindy said sympathetically.

The flat that just a couple of days earlier I'd finally decided that I could call 'home' now resembled a refuse tip. The contents of the kitchen cupboards were strewn all over the floor. All the packets of food had been emptied out, the empty packets casually discarded. In the living area the stuffing had been pulled from the sofa and heaped on the carpet. The bedding had been removed from the bed; the comforter ripped apart so that the filling blew around in the draught from the door and the stuffing from the mattress and the pillow joined the rest of the discarded mess on the floor. Even the carpet had been pulled up around the edges.

I took a step forward and picked up the remains of the shredded comforter, folded it neatly and put it on top of the television. I noticed that the back of the television had been taken off.

"Anything taken?" Nat asked, coming to stand beside me and flinging his arm round my shoulder.

I shook my head. "I've no idea." I walked around. The kettle and the toaster were both still where I'd left them, and they were the most valuable things in the flat.

What did that say about my life?

"I don't think so."

Cindy had disappeared from the flat and she reappeared now. "Cops are on their way," she said. "I told them that you'll be next door with me." Her eyes roamed round the room. "Seems like they were looking for something."

I decided that I'd rather assume that the destruction had been a deliberate act in the search for something rather than just random vandalism.

"I don't know what," I said, "I haven't got anything worth taking." My voice was unsteady and I suspected that tears weren't far away.

Cindy took my arm and the three of us left the room. At the door I turned back and looked, still unable to believe my eyes.

"Come on, hun." Nat took my other arm and led me into Cindy's apartment.

"You can stay here tonight," Cindy said. "I've got a spare mattress."

"No, that's all right," I sobbed, "I'll go home."

"Home? I assume you mean your apartment rather than England? You can't go back there. It'll take days just to sort the place out. No, you can stay with me tonight and we'll rethink in the morning." Cindy was adamant and it didn't look as though I was going to change her mind. Truthfully I didn't really want to.

"Thanks." I managed, my voice weak with shock and tears.

"You're welcome. You working tonight, Nat?"

"Nope. Next gig's Friday, at Molly Malone's."

Cindy looked at the clock. "I'm due at the club in a couple of hours.
I've called and told them I might be late but I'll still have to leave as soon as
the cops have been. Okay if Laura spends the evening with you, and I'll pick
her up after work?"

"Sure."

I began to feel like a child being baby-sat. "Hey, look, I don't want
to be a burden…"

"You're not. Don't be silly." Cindy patted my hand. "You're
welcome to stay here if you want, but I'll be at work and I thought that you
might like some company."

"And I'd like it if you'd come round." Nat said. "We could get a
pizza and watch a movie or something."

"Haven't you got anything better to do?" I asked him, worried that I
might be treading on one of his many girlfriends' toes.

"Not tonight. Got a hot date lined up for tomorrow," he grinned,
"but no takers for tonight."

"Okay, then, if you're sure." I looked from one to the other of them.
"Thanks, guys."

I had to go back into the flat when the police came. And Cindy, Nat
and I all had our fingers dusted for the purpose of elimination.

It was nasty in the flat. I knew now what people meant when they
said they felt that they'd been violated following a break in. They'd been
through my underwear, for God's sake. I'd have to wash all my undies
before I wore them now; I couldn't bear the thought of fabric they'd touched
touching my skin. Ugh. In fact I might have to actually throw this stuff and
buy new. No, I couldn't afford that, a good wash would have to suffice.

The cop that took my statement suggested that dusting for
fingerprints may not be very rewarding. There had been a lot of people
through the flat. I did point out that every surface in the flat had been
scrubbed since I moved in so the only fingerprints found in the flat should be
Nat, Cindy's, Sara's and mine. The cop told me that I'd be surprised how
many fingerprints would have escaped my cleaning and *I* told *him* that he'd
be surprised how thorough a clean the flat had received. Stalemate.

Once I'd given my statement I left the police to it and told them
they'd find me in Nat's flat if they needed me. I also suggested that if they

wanted to talk to Cindy then they'd better catch her soon before she left for work.

I didn't even bother to pick up my pj's, I'd be sleeping in the underwear I had on tonight; at least I could be sure that nobody else had been touching them.

Cindy called in at Nat's on her way to work. I hardly recognised her with her hair pinned up and make up on. I had thought she was pretty before, but now she was stunning.

"I've got the mattress out and made up a bed for you," she said. "If Nat gets too much for you then you can bed down any time you want, Nat's got a key to my apartment. Otherwise I'll catch you here when I get home."

I tried to thank her, but she hushed me "It's what friends are for."

Nat and I slobbed out that evening. We scoffed Pizza, chocolate ice cream and a couple of cream cakes that Nat found in the ice box in his 'fridge, nuking them because we didn't want to wait until they thawed out. There were crisps – or chips as Nat called them although to me chips were something quite different – as well, and peanuts, and by the time Cindy returned from work I'd eaten so much that I felt as though I was about to explode.

Nat and I had watched movies and, in-between, made small talk about nothing important. Nat seemed intent on keeping my mind off the break-in as though it had been a great tragedy that I should try and block out.

It wasn't a tragedy, I knew that. Nobody had died (I didn't dare consider what might have happened to me if I'd walked in on the intruders) and I hadn't lost anything of value – mainly because there wasn't anything of any worth in the flat. I'd have to speak to Con about replacing the mattress and the sofa – presumably he had insurance – but that could be a blessing in disguise. I wondered if I could get a new carpet out of it as well. I was upset about the curtains but I'd had a look at them and didn't think they were irreparable. The inconvenience was the biggest problem. I couldn't stay with Cindy forever and I didn't know how I was going to feel about being alone in the flat now.

"You'll be okay," Cindy said when she came home from work and I voiced my fears. "When you're inside the flat you've got all those bolts and chains on the door. Nobody will be *able* to get in then."

"I've only got one bolt and one chain," I pointed out, "but I take your point. It's when I'm out that the flat is vulnerable."

Cindy, unlike Nat, seemed to think that it was better for me to talk about the break-in and get all my worries aired. Maybe she was right, I don't know.   Whatever, the three of us sat up drinking coffee (Nat and I had already sunk a few beers by the time Cindy returned) and talking the remainder of the night away.

"Do you think that this break-in was anything to do with Russ?" I asked at one point.

Cindy and Nat exchanged glances. "Could be," Nat said eventually. "I wouldn't have brought it up but given that the door's been broken down before it does make you wonder. And we never had any trouble until Russ moved in and since then we've had two break-ins, both at the same flat."

"We ought to get in the habit of locking the street door," Cindy said.

Everyone resident in the block had a key for the street door but it was seldom locked. As I'd been told when I'd done my research, the area enjoyed a very low crime rate and nobody expected to experience a break in. Plus everybody had their own security on their own apartments of course.

"Maybe we ought to print up some flyers and distribute them round the other tenants?" I suggested. "Let them know about the break-ins and suggest that we keep the outer door locked. They'd probably let me print some up at work."

Nat nodded. "Good idea, hun."

"So Russ must have had something that somebody is looking for?" I said.

Cindy and Nat both nodded. "It looks like it." Nat said.

"What do you actually *know* about Russ?" I asked.

"Very little," Cindy said, "in fact you probably know more than we do. I didn't know, for instance, about the girlfriend."

"What? You'd not seen her here at the flat with Russ?"

"I hadn't, certainly. What about you, Nat?"

Nat shook his head. "No, but that's not that strange. We really don't see many comings and goings unless we happen to pass on the stairs. And the walls are so thick that you don't hear if your neighbours have company. She could have been there loads of times and we wouldn't necessary know."

"And Russ did tend to keep himself to himself," Cindy said. "I'd see him occasionally – often he'd be coming home when I left for work in the evening. He was friendly enough if we *did* meet, would stop and chat for a while, but we didn't actually *socialise* with him, did we, Nat?"

"I hardly spoke to him all the time he was there," Nat said.

"We knocked on his door the day he moved in," Cindy said, "the same as we did for you and he was friendly enough, but wouldn't take the wine and didn't invite us in. I never saw inside the apartment while he was there, did you, Nat?"

"Nope. Never did."

"Sara said he was some sort of salesman. Do you know what he sold?"

They both shook their heads.

"What do you think they could have been looking for," I asked. "It must have been something quite small if they thought it might be hidden between the lining and the curtain."

"Could have been a photograph, or a CD or DVD p'raps," Nat suggested. "Or money."

"Or maybe they didn't know *what* they were looking for," Cindy said, "and were just ripping everything up in case."

I shivered.

"Don't worry, hun," Nat patted my arm, "they've searched everywhere now, they've no reason to come back."

Perhaps he was right but for tonight, at least, I was glad not to be sleeping in my flat.

It was three o'clock by the time I tumbled onto the mattress that Cindy had prepared for me in her apartment. Within seconds I was asleep.

CHAPTER SIX

I spent another two nights on the mattress in Cindy's apartment.

I called work the day following the break in and told them that I was sick. It wasn't a lie; I had a thumping headache by then, probably partly due to the alcohol that I'd consumed the previous night but more than likely more due to the stress. Whatever, I woke with the headache the following day and it didn't begin to get better until I'd drunk several black coffees and eaten half a dozen doughnuts. "Guaranteed to make you feel better," Cindy promised as she put the bag of doughnuts on the kitchen table.

Cindy amazed me. Granted she'd not been drinking all night the way that Nat and I had but she didn't get to bed until three this morning - the same as me, yet she was chipper as a sparrow at nine the next day and had already been to the bakers. *And* she'd picked me up a pack of new pants. She must have had about four hours sleep yet she looked fresh as a daisy.

It wasn't just today either. She rolled in most nights between one and two in the morning, yet I often passed her coming back from the shops when I was on my way out to work. I wished that I had half her stamina.

Breakfast finished we started tidying the flat – or trying to. I knew that the police had been in touch with Con the previous evening and he'd promised to send someone round today to assess the situation.

The damage was superficial but it was still daunting. Cindy bundled some clothes in my arms and pressed some loose change in my hand and sent me down to the basement. "Go on," she said, "I know that you want to wash everything."

How right she was. In the basement several people that I knew vaguely by sight came up and offered their sympathy on the break in. It was amazing how news had travelled so quickly round the building. An elderly lady offered me the spare bed in her apartment, which I thanked her for and explained that I was sleeping at a friend's. I would have been more likely to accept *her* offer though than the one I got from a hairy, flat-faced individual who leered at me and asked if I'd like to share *his* bed.

I left the clothes in the washer and returned to the flat. Cindy had cleared the floor already – things damaged beyond repair were piled into black bags and the rest of the stuff was stacked on the kitchen units. In reality I didn't have that many possessions in the first place but, like spilt milk, it had looked a lot when spread about the floor. My new kettle and the toaster were undamaged. I was surprised that the intruders hadn't taken them to pieces and grateful that they hadn't. Perhaps their very newness indicated that they were too new to have been there in Russ's time.

"Right. Coffee," Cindy said, and we trooped back to her flat.

"You can sleep here until Con sorts you out a new mattress," Cindy said as she placed a steaming cup of coffee in front of me.

Today Cindy was wearing a pair of old, frayed jeans and a big, polo neck jumper. Somewhat different to her work clothes – a skimpy pair of pants that were little more than a thong, together with a narrow strip of material across her breasts – or boobies, as she was inclined to refer to them. It was funny how Cindy managed to fit well in both personas. Looking at her now she was just "the girl next door" and you couldn't imagine her looking glamorous, yet if you didn't know her and you saw her in her work clothes you would imagine she was the sort of woman that never looked *less* than immaculate. And somehow, even when dressed for work, Cindy never looked tarty; her face held a look of innocence which probably – I didn't know her well enough to say – belied the woman within.

I suppose that we all have many facets to our personalities but others only see what we choose to show them.

I know that a lot of my old work-mates back in the UK were gobsmacked when I upped and relocated to Alaska. They knew I came from a close family and were amazed that I'd want to leave them. I hadn't *wanted* to leave them; of course, it was more that I needed to be with Glen. Other friends – those who knew me well, were gobsmacked to see me blindly following some man across the world. They – and I – had always thought that I would always be the one in control in any relationship. Falling for Glen the way I had was completely out of character, and so was the way I turned a blind eye to his faults – faults that were so obvious to everyone else. I suppose that's what love does to you.

I looked round Cindy's apartment now. It was roughly the same size as mine and, with a mattress on the floor, there was barely room to move.

"Are you sure?" I asked, knowing that if she changed her mind about me staying then I'd really be in bother.

"Course I'm sure," she grinned. "It'll work out okay. You'll be at work during the day and I'll be at work in the evenings, so we won't crowd each other. And when we're both here we can have girlie chats. It'll only be for a few days anyway, just until Con sorts you out a new mattress. And if by any chance it did run into the weekend then you'll have this flat to yourself as Tony and I are off to stay with friends for a couple of nights."

I thanked Cindy and told her that I really hoped to be back in my own place by the weekend.

Con turned up himself later that day to assess the damage. He complained about the state of the sofa and mattress as though it was *my* fault that they had been rendered useless.

"The insurance doesn't cover you for the personal stuff you've lost," he pointed out. "You'll have to replace the food yourself. But I suppose I'll have to find you a new mattress and sofa."

"Yes, I think that you will. It's part of the agreement that the flat is furnished."

"When I say 'new'," he said, "I don't actually mean *new*, just new to you. "

My heart sank. I'd been hoping for brand new. Stupid me, I should have known better. Even if Con had a "new for old" policy he was more likely to pocket the money and buy second hand than he was to actually provide his tenants with new furniture. Still, in view of the lack of contract, it had been a bit risky of me to mention an agreement, so anything I got was welcome.

"What about the carpet?" I asked. Surely he could stretch to a new carpet for the room?

He shrugged. "I'll get my man to re-lay it,"

"What? You're going to re-lay this, not get a new one?"

He bent down and ran his hand across the pile – well, "pile" is a bit of an exaggeration, it was more like a piece of board.

"Nothing wrong with that." He said, straightening up. "We'll just get the edges tacked down again."

I looked at him in wonderment. "If this carpet was on your floor at home, would *you* just tack it down or would you replace it?"

"Oh, I'd replace it," he said without hesitation. "But then I'm not desperate for somewhere to live, am I? Of course," he moved a step closer to me, bent his head down to my level and his frown turned to a *leer,* "Of course," he said again, "you might like to stay with me for a little while. After all, you are nearly family."

In that case what he'd got in mind would be incest. What was it with men? As soon as they thought a woman was vulnerable then they thought she wouldn't be able to stop herself falling into their strong, manly arms. Like I said before, an offer like that from Con was *not* an appealing thought.

"Just get me the things." I said, turning on my heel. "And have them here by Friday."

I opened the door and waited for him to leave.

"I'll get them here when I want to," he muttered as he walked past me on to the landing.

"In that case my rent will be reduced accordingly as the facilities aren't complete" I shouted after him.

He turned round and glared, before heading for the stairs.

I really must stop upsetting Con or I'd find myself out on the street. Still, it was satisfying to show him that I wasn't the walkover that he appeared to think I was. I supposed that I must have seemed that way to him when I was bawling in his car. Well, he knew differently now.

Nat surfaced in the early afternoon and came round to see what he could do to help. By that time the flat was back to as near normal as we could get it. I was in Cindy's sewing the lining back on my curtains and Cindy was down in the basement collecting the final batch of my washing.

"Oh, I've missed it all then, have I?" Nat asked.

"You have," I told him, "although we're probably due for another coffee if you want to put the kettle on." I nodded in the direction of the kitchen and he headed off and put the kettle on to boil."

"You okay?" he asked, coming back and sitting beside me on Cindy's sofa.

I put the sewing down and thought about it. Was I okay?

"Yes. Yes, I am." I told Nat eventually. I picked up the sewing again. "I don't like the idea that people were in my flat going through my things, but I'm pretty sure that it wasn't personal. I believe that whatever they were after had more to do with Russ Bracken than Laura Evans. And, as Cindy says, they know now that whatever they're after isn't in the flat so they won't be back." I smiled at Nat. "Hopefully."

"I'm sure that they won't, hun," Nat gave me a quick hug and went off to make the coffee.

"I've put the washing on top of the chest in your apartment," Cindy said, coming through the door. "Did I hear Nat's voice?"

"You certainly did." Nat came out of the kitchen with the coffee.

"Great, I'm parched." Cindy took her coffee and sat on the bed. "How about we go over to Terry's for dinner?" she asked.

Terry's was a diner on the square outside the apartment block. I'd eaten there on a couple of occasions and it was an okay place. Today though, when I'd got to replace nearly everything in my store cupboard, I didn't really think I could afford to eat out, however cheap and cheerful Terry's was.

41

"Oh, I don't think —" I began."

"It's not like you've got any food in, have you?" Cindy pointed out.

No, that was true, I didn't have any food left in my cupboard. There had been a couple of tomatoes in the 'fridge and some eggs and milk, but I'd thrown everything away — I didn't know whose hands might have touched anything or who might have spat in the milk. I'd been hoping to scrounge a sandwich from Cindy or Nat.

Cindy and Nat exchanged glances and Nat nodded. What was that about, I wondered?

"That's settled then," Cindy said. "And it's our treat."

"Not that going to Terry's is exactly a *treat,*" Nat said, "but it's on us."

Tears pricked my eyes. My eyes were doing a lot of leaking just lately

"Oh, I couldn't," I said.

"Course you could," Cindy said. "Are you going back to work tomorrow?"

I nodded. "I've no reason not to and the quicker I can get back to something approaching normal the better."

"I'll stock up the cupboards for you then," she said. "Make me a list tonight."

"Oh, would you, that'd be great. Thanks, Cindy."

Nat asked me if I wanted to spend the evening with him again while Cindy was at work. I remembered that he'd said yesterday that he had a "hot date" for tonight so declined his offer. I didn't want to play gooseberry and I certainly didn't want him letting down his date just because he felt I needed company.

When Cindy arrived home in the early hours I was already fast asleep on the mattress, dreaming of England and summer.

CHAPTER SEVEN

November blew out in a huge snowstorm. Six or seven inches fell in one night and I found myself longing for summer.

That amount of snow falling in one go back home would have disrupted the whole of England – hell, even three or four inches would have prevented people turning up for work. Here everything went on as normal. The snowploughs had cleared the main thoroughfares by the time I set off for work and I was grateful to find that the pavements had been cleared as well.

My route to work took me past the hotel that my parents had booked into for their Christmas trip. Mum had told me which hotel they would be staying in and I'd been and checked it out. In fact Maisie and I "took tea" in their dining room one Saturday afternoon. The staff were friendly and helpful, they even showed us round some of the rooms that were empty when I told them my parents would be staying there. The rooms were warm, pretty and well equipped, and the food that they served us for tea was excellent.

My biggest worry now was that bad weather might disrupt their flight – that or a strike by aircrew or something. Bad weather wouldn't upset things this end. Like I said, Alaskans were always prepared for heavy snow, but if a centimetre fell at Heathrow then all bets could be off. Okay, so that's an exaggeration – just, but now I was so looking forward to seeing them that I felt sure that something would go wrong. Of course, I'd still have the trauma of them discovering how I was living, but I'd resigned myself to that and it was outweighed now by the anticipation of seeing Mum and Dad.

I'd got myself a bit of extra money together by singing with Nat's band. In an unusual display of opportune moments, fate had stepped in and taken a hand.

Nat announced one evening that his band were looking for a singer, their current singer was six months pregnant and was finding that standing on a stage belting out songs for several hours was getting too much for her. She was hoping to rejoin the band after the baby was born, but they wanted someone to fill in while she took "maternity leave". I'd mentioned to Nat at some point that I sang in choirs back home and he asked me if I'd be interested in filling in. It turned out that they'd been looking for months and hadn't found anybody suitable. There was no guarantee that I'd be suitable either, of course, so I went along to a rehearsal one weekend, hit it off with the guys in the band, and I was in.

Excellent. It meant that I could shop for Christmas pressies now without eating into the "going home fund".

"We've had some right odd lassies audition," Alastair, the Scottish bass player told me, "and some right old women as well."

"From Alastair's perspective 25 looks old," Nat told me. "He's only 17, but he plays a mean guitar. Anyway, we've only seen four applicants. And, honestly, age wasn't a factor. If the 45-year-old woman had fitted, we'd have been just as happy having her front the bad. She had a beautiful voice, sharp and clear, like crystal piercing steel." He shrugged. "We're a rock band. We don't need clarity, we need guts and power."

As it happened they decided that I had both, which is how I found myself in a dark alley behind the hall in which we'd been performing. The rest of the band was still knocking back drinks and I was making a start on loading up the van. Usually we all sat around unwinding with a drink after a gig, but tonight I felt restless, so I left the rest of them to it. Besides, it was a Sunday night and some of us had to be up for work in the morning. I reckoned that if I could load up the smaller stuff then it would save time.

It wasn't a van really, it was more of a 4 x 4 truck, so everything was loaded on to the back and then strapped in and covered with a tarpaulin. Nat and I travelled in the cab with Gene, the driver, while the other two band members travelled to gigs independently. The drum kit, amps and similar paraphernalia all "lived" at Gene's' house.

I was leaning over the truck, packing mike stands carefully down one side when a hand was laid on my shoulder.

I jumped and spun round, to be confronted by two hulking great men. The light in the alley was dim, but I could see that the goon that was standing closest to me had a scar down the side of his face and a nose that pretty much filled the rest of it.

"Where's Russ?" the goon demanded.

My mind went blank – well, whose wouldn't? "Russ?" My voice caught in my throat and I coughed.

"Russ Bracken. You must know where he is."

"What the hell -?" Suddenly I just saw red. What the hell were these goons doing questioning me as to the whereabouts of someone that I'd never met – someone who'd already caused me enough grief? I pushed the guy away – well, I laid my hands on his chest and shoved, but it didn't seem to make a lot of difference.

"I don't *know* Russ," I spat. "I just happen to be living where he used to live. He's not living there now. *I* am." A thought struck me. "Are you the idiots that broke in to my apartment and trashed it?"

44

I didn't see it coming. A hand connected to the side of my face and I fell back against the truck.

"Now perhaps you'll tell us what you know," Goon number two said, stepping round the side of Big Nose.

I was too busy feeling pain to reply immediately. My hand had automatically gone to my jaw and I tried to move it around a bit, the way I'd seen them do in the films. I think the idea was to see if the jaw had been dislocated. I didn't think it had. It hurt like hell though. Experimentally, I opened my mouth and wiggled my jaw. Everything seemed to be working normally.

I stepped forward. I would *not* show that I was afraid. "You've got the wrong person," I said.

Goon number two stepped towards me until he was so close that I could feel his breath on my face and I could smell the fish he had for tea. "Where is he?" he demanded, spitting in my face. "Where's Russ Bracken?" I recoiled from the halitosis breath and hit my head against the truck.

"Ow," I rubbed the back of my head.

Goon number two turned to Big Nose goon. "She don't know nothin'. Take her out."

What was going on? Suddenly I seemed to have been transported to the set of a B movie.

Even Big Nose looked puzzled.

"Huh?"

"Beat her up a bit. Let them see we mean business, " Goon number two said.

"Oh, okay."

It suddenly dawned on me that these guys intended to do me some serious damage and I darted past Goon number two, heading for the door of the hall. Big Nose was too quick for me and caught me from behind, wrapping his arms across my chest in a vice like grip.

"Not so fast, little lady."

He twisted me round, pulled his arm back in preparation for punching me in the face, and I brought my knee up between his legs.

Hard.

It wasn't a move I'd ever been able to practice before – you don't get many men volunteering to be the victim, so I didn't know if it was going to work. I didn't stay around to find out though; as soon as he uttered a cry like a dog yelping and his grip on my arm weakened I spun round and flew towards the door. I could hear the goons' footsteps behind me and I barged through the swing door into the bar area,

The guys from the band all turned when the door smashed against the wall as I shot through it.

"What the -?"

All three stood up. Gene was nearest, and Gene stood 6'6" and was nearly as broad as he was tall – okay, so that's another exaggeration, but he was solid muscle, and there was a lot of him.

I heard the goons skid to a halt behind me but I carried on running. I fetched up next to Nat, who put an arm round me and pulled me to him. "You okay, hun?"

I looked up at him and smiled. I knew that it was a trembly smile, but it *was* a smile.

Nat looked towards the door. "Who the –?" The goons were only there but a second or two. They took one look at Gene and fled.

"Want us to go after them?" Gene asked.

I shook my head, "No, let them go. No point in carrying this on or risking anyone getting hurt."

Gene looked as though he was about to argue.

"Please," I begged. I couldn't bear it if any of the band got hurt in my defence.

"Best go and check the van though," Nat said.

Gene nodded and headed out to the alley.

I wondered if that was Nat's way of letting me think they were abiding by my wishes while actually hunting down the goons, but I couldn't protest; it was right that they check the van, and keep an eye on it.

"So what was all that about?" Adam, the bartender walked out from behind the bar and handed me a small glass. "Drink," he commanded.

I knocked back the brandy and felt its warmth spread through my body.

"They thought I knew where someone that they were looking for was." I looked at Nat. "Russ."

"No way!" Nat looked as flabbergasted as I felt.

"Why?" I asked. "What's Russ got that they want? And why pick on *me?*"

Despite the warmth of the brandy I shivered. In fact, I was shaking all over. Nat, who still had his arm round me, obviously felt this. "Sit down," he said, "come on, over here." He pulled up a chair and gently lowered me into it.

"Shock," said Adam and produced a blanket from under the bar, which he wrapped round my shoulder. I was to wonder later *why* there'd been a blanket there. The answer was obvious though; it got cold here in Alaska and if any of the bar staff couldn't get home for any reason, a blanket or two would come in very handy.

"You've got a nasty bruise coming up there," Nat said, running a finger across my jaw.

"One of the thugs hit me," I said, giving way to the tears that had been threatening.

"What?" Alastair was on his way through the door when Adam called him back.

"They'll be long gone," he said, "Waste of time. Besides, Gene is out there, he'd have let us know if they were still about." He turned to Nat. "Should we take her to hospital?"

"Hun?"

I shook my head, "No, I'm okay," I sobbed. "Sorry."

Nat squeezed my arm. "Don't be silly."

Gene came back at that moment and I saw him shake his head. I guessed that meant that the Goons were long gone. That didn't make me feel any better though.

"They were going to beat me up," I wailed.

"So how did you get away?"

"I kneed him in the nuts," I snuffled, a smile breaking through the tears.

"You did *what?*" Nat kissed my cheek "Good on ya. Well done."

Alastair and Adam broke out in spontaneous applause.

"No wonder they ran," Adam said.

"I don't think it was that," I sniffed, "I think it was more likely the sight of you yobs."

"Yobs?"

"Well, look at you," I said, my voice weak but coherent, "You all look pretty hard. I reckon that they realised they were outnumbered and decided that discretion was the better part of valour."

"Maybe," Adam said, pulling out his cell 'phone. "I'm calling the cops."

I could see my night's sleep slipping away. I put a hand on Adam's arm. "Don't," I said. "They'll keep us up all night if you do. Look, nobody's hurt, not really. I'll give them a ring tomorrow and tell them."

"Can you describe the men who attacked you?" Nat asked.

I nodded. "Oh, yes, don't worry. The light was dim but I got a good enough look at them."

"Well, I still think that we ought to call the police now," Adam said. "What do you think, Nat?"

Nat looked from me to Adam and back again. "I agree, we *ought* to call the cops, but I think Laura's had enough for one night. Let's get her home."

Relieved, I sank back against Nat. "Thanks, mate," I said.

"Okay," Adam agreed, albeit reluctantly. "The attackers are probably miles away by now anyway."

"Everything seemed okay in the van." Gene said. "I looked around but couldn't see anyone hanging about, so I think whoever it was is long gone by now."

"Come on, let's get the rest of the gear packed up," Alastair said, "and then you can get Laura home."

"I'll give you a hand." Adam headed for the stage and Nat, Gene and Alastair followed him. "You stay here," Nat said. "No need for you to do anything."

I stood up and tested my legs. A bit like jelly, but I thought that they would hold my weight okay. "I'd rather help, Nat. Help take my mind off things."

"If you're sure."

It didn't take us long to pack all the gear away.

"You make sure you call the cops first thing, okay?" was Adam's parting shot. "We don't want those two thugs running around if we can help it, the quicker they're put away the better."

I knew, and I'm sure that Adam knew as well, that the two men who had attacked me were unlikely to get caught and even if they were they wouldn't necessarily be put away, it would depend on whether they had a record. Mind you, I was pretty sure that the police wouldn't have to dig too far to find something on the two goons I'd encountered in the alley.

"You going to be okay on your own tonight?" Nat asked as we climbed the stairs in the apartment block. "You could always spend the night with me."

"Oh, Nat, this is so sudden." I grinned at him.

"No, no, I didn't mean – not that I wouldn't of course. Oh, I shouldn't have said that - not that I didn't mean it, I mean," Nat hit his forehead with the heel of his hand. "Sheesh, I'm digging myself a hole here. What I meant to say was if you'd rather have company you could take my bed and I'd sleep on the couch. Or," and a slow smile spread across his face, "if you were feeling *really* lonely we could both take the bed."

Luckily I knew Nat well enough by now to know he was joking.

I rolled my eyes. "That's really kind of you, Nat, but I can't let these thugs win. Besides, once I'm in and all the locks are on I'm sure I'll be pretty safe."

We reached our floor and Nat stood by me while I unlocked my door. He wouldn't let me go in until he'd checked the flat was completely empty.

"Keep your cell by your bed," he said when he left, "and ring me if you need me, even if you just feel lonely." He winked. "I'll come running."

"Go on with you." I pushed him out of the flat. "I'll be fine."

I watched him walk along the corridor to his apartment. "Oh, and Nat –"

He turned round.

"Thanks for looking out for me."

"You're very welcome, hun. 'Night." He blew me an air-kiss and disappeared into his apartment

CHAPTER EIGHT

Cindy was hammering on my door when I came out of the shower the following morning. I opened the door with the chain on, but took it off when I saw who it was.

She burst in. "What's this I hear about you being beaten up?" she demanded.

"I really wasn't beaten up, Cindy," I protested. "The worst that happened was a slap in the face."

She came up and peered at me. "Yeah. Nat said there was a bruise, and there is. It must have been a pretty hefty slap then."

She didn't need to tell me about the bruise, I'd spotted it for myself. No amount of concealer was going to completely hide it either, I'd spent hours putting the stuff on and covering it with face powder – something I didn't normally use (I had some because I'd raided Mum's make-up drawer before I left home – goodness knows why I'd added the powder to my hoard though). Anyway, the powder didn't reduce the look of the bruise *at all!*

And although I made light of the attack, I'd spent a very restless night thinking about what *might* have happened. I was just glad that I'd managed to react and not been frozen with fear. If I hadn't acted quickly then I could have been lying in a bloody mess on the ground by the time the guys came out to pack the band gear away. I guess it could have gone either way and I was just lucky – or maybe it's in my nature to act before thinking.

"Have you called the cops?" Cindy asked.

"Yes, they've got someone in the area and he's coming round to interview me this morning." I didn't add that I'd been given a right bollocking by the voice at the end of the 'phone for not having contacted them the night before.

I'd called work as well and let them know I'd be in later. Although the firm operated flexi-hours we were supposed to be there each working day for the core hours – 10 a.m. until 4 p.m. and I suspected I wouldn't make the 10 o'clock start that morning.

I'd 'phoned Sara, too, and told her of the latest developments. "Don't go out on your own," I told her, "And by 'not on your own' I don't mean with Tommy, I mean have another adult with you, preferably your Dad." Sara's dad was small and wiry and had been trained in the army. I knew, because he had told me the day I'd spent at their house, that he could break a man's neck with a single blow and I thought that was probably the kind of protection Sara needed.

I'd enjoyed the day that I'd spent with Sara. Her parents had made me very welcome and Sara and I had lounged about, watching music videos and chatting. Sara's Mum even took over looking after Tommy most of the day. The whole day just made me miss being part of a family group.

Sara's parents had, naturally, been worried silly about Russ' disappearance and they questioned me considerably as to whether I had any clue where he might have gone. Soon it became obvious that I knew as little as they did about Russ' whereabouts and they left Sara and I alone then, to enjoy the day and just relax.

So far whoever was after Russ didn't appear to have latched on to Sara. For some reason they were focussed on the flat and, by association, me. We'd worked out that last night's thugs must have followed the van when Gene picked Nat and me up, and hung around waiting for an opportunity to jump me.

Sara had been upset that I had been the one who had been attacked. "It doesn't seem fair that they should pick on you when you didn't even *know* Russ. At least there would have been some kind of justice if it had been me who had been attacked. At least I *knew* him."

I'd pointed out that if Sara had been the one that they picked on then they might have hurt Tommy as well, and the thought of anyone hurting that cute little baby just didn't bear thinking about.

"If they don't know of your existence then let's keep it that way," I said. "Best if you don't come to the apartment any more, they may be watching the flat to clock all the comings and goings and I don't want them spotting you. I just think we're lucky that they don't seem to know about you already."

"To be honest, Laura," Sara said, "I only went to the apartment a couple of times. It was so small, you know, and poky. Sorry, I don't mean to be rude about your home but it was just easier if Russ came here when we were together."

"Yeah, I can understand that." Sara's parents lived in the "posh" part of town. Their five bed-roomed house boasted a balcony overlooking a lake. Not that there was much to see this time of year, just a lot of snow but the view in summer must be spectacular.

"You don't think that my 'phone's bugged, do you?" I asked, suddenly nervous.

"Now you're being stupid," Sara said, "I refuse to even consider the possibility."

Sara's confidence made me feel better. "Have you heard back from anyone?" I asked.

A couple of weeks ago Sara and I had got together and composed letters to both Russ' ex-wife and his friend, James, who had sent the letter that we'd opened the first day Sara and I met. They'd been difficult letters to compose. We thought about being completely open and saying that Sara was Russ' girlfriend and that we were worried as Russ seemed to have disappeared, but we didn't know Russ' ex wife, and didn't know how she'd feel about there being another woman in his life. She might automatically clam up and not tell us anything. If she and James were in contact – and it stood to reason that if Russ and James had known one another that long then somewhere along the line Russ' wife and James had probably met – then she might convince James not to tell us anything either. The other side of the coin was that, judging by the tone of her letters, she was obviously still fond of Russ despite their separation and we didn't want to alarm her unduly. After all, we didn't know that anything *had* happened to Russ, we were just trying to find out if James or Russ' ex had seen him recently.

In the end we decided to pose as the wife of a friend of Russ' who was trying to contact Russ to invite him to a surprise party that she was arranging for her husband.

No replies had been forthcoming so far, we just had to sit and wait a bit longer.

The officer who came to interview me was the same one who'd taken my statement after the break-in. I remembered that his name was Chris Harrington, mainly because Cindy had talked about him. She'd been in the same year as him at school and told me that when they first left school Chris had gone off the rails a bit. She'd lost touch with him and then he'd suddenly turned up in the paper winning some police award or other.

"He's obviously "found" himself, whatever that means," Cindy had said. "Good. He was a nice kid and I wouldn't like to have seen him go to waste. I've seen him recently and he's turned into a good-looking, kind guy."

Today a female officer accompanied him. He introduced her as Cherryl Kramer. She nodded at me but didn't say anything.

Chris took down the details of the attack. "You're sure you're okay?" he asked as he closed his notebook. "We can provide counselling, you know, if you think that it would help."

52

"I'm fine," I said. "I just wish that this Russ would turn up, then perhaps they'd stop hassling me."

"Hmm, I'll check when I get back to the department and see how that's going." Sara had reported Russ' apparent disappearance the day after she'd shown up at my flat for the first time. She said they hadn't seemed very interested. Russ was, after all, a grown man and at the time hadn't really been gone long enough to be considered 'missing'.

Chris shrugged. "There's a limit to how much manpower we put in when a grown man disappears, but seeing as his no-show is having this kind of repercussion we may be inclined to dig a bit deeper. In the meantime," he got up from the sofa and headed for the door, closely followed by his colleague who had yet to say anything, "keep the door locked and don't let any strangers in."

"I won't," I promised, and I bolted the door behind them and put the chain on.

"Well, that went well," I said to myself as I leaned back against the door. "I think it achieved absolutely nothing." There was no way they'd ever come up with my attacker and okay, they might have another look at their "missing persons" file but, as Chris Harrington had said, they weren't going to put a lot of time on searching for a grown man, especially as they had no proof that the attack on my flat and on my person were connected to Russ' disappearance.

I sighed and went and made myself a coffee and I sat at the breakfast bar to drink it. Well, the term "breakfast bar" was probably rather grander than the bit of wood stuck on the wall deserved. I had decided that I wanted somewhere to sit where I could have a surface on which to write, or somewhere just to eat a meal. I'd purchased a piece of wood and some hinges and, with Cindy's help, had managed to fix the wood to the wall. It folded down when not in use and I was actually quite proud of my DIY attempt. I'd picked up a pair of kitchen stools in a garage sale and now I, and a friend if I had a visitor, could sit comfortably with a coffee or a meal.

I pulled a writing pad from the small bookcase behind the sofa and took a pen from my purse. At the top of the page I wrote "Russ Bracken".

Beneath his name I wrote "Last known address" and my apartment address beside it. On the next line I put "known contacts" and wrote Sara's name and location, then added Russ' ex-wife and James. I didn't know their addresses because Sara had the original letters but I could add them later.

I tapped my teeth with my pen while I considered what else we knew about Russ. Not a lot, I decided.

On the next few lines I wrote "Employers", "Hobbies", and "any other information". I didn't think that Sara had ever actually mentioned the name of Russ' employers but she must know it because she'd 'phoned them, hadn't she?

I didn't know how knowing Russ' hobbies would help, but it might lead us to some other contacts; it was something that I'd have to speak to Sara about.

On the next page I made a note of the break in and the attack on me last night. I noted Chris Harrington's name down as the officer that I'd had contact with, just in case I needed it. However, I *knew* Chris Harrington's name so why did I need to write it down? Obviously my subconscious had decided that it was in case anything happened to me. The officer who investigated my untimely death would be able to liase with Chris and save himself or herself some legwork. And did thoughts of my untimely death bother me? You bet!

I checked my watch and decided that it was time to leave for work. I'd make up my late start at the end of the day.

When Nat had dropped me off the previous evening he'd offered to walk into work with me and meet me on the way home. It was a really kind offer, especially from someone who didn't normally surface until mid-afternoon, but I told him that it really wasn't necessary, and that I thought I'd convinced the attackers that I really didn't know Russ' whereabouts and that they'd leave me alone now.

I hoped I was right. I could remember one of the guys saying "show them we mean business." I'm not sure who the "them" was that he was referring to, but I understood the threat. And maybe there was no "them" but he just liked seeing people suffer. He seemed like the kind of guy who could get a good deal of pleasure from watching another's pain.

I squared my shoulders and let myself out of the flat. Chris Harrington had said that they'd have someone keeping an eye on the house. I think that he just meant that when they cruised by down the street they'd cast half a glance in the direction of my apartment, but it was comforting just the same.

For the next few days I felt nervous every time I stepped out of the house, even if I was with a friend, as I was with Maisie on the Friday evening. By then though, I was beginning to believe that maybe I *had* seen the last of them and that perhaps the streets were safe for me to walk again.

CHAPTER NINE

Mum and Dad arrived the Saturday before Christmas. I hired a car to go and pick them up from the airport. I knew they'd be knackered after the flight so I'd decided that I would put off telling them about Glen and me until after they had rested.

"And then you'll find another excuse," Cindy said when I told her what I planned. "You're going to have to tell them sometime, Laura."

"Yes, and I *will* tell them. Just as soon as I can."

I knew I *had* to tell them, but I was worried now that they might be angry I hadn't told them when it happened and saved them the cost of the fare. A little voice was telling me that they might also be hurt by my not turning to them when I was in trouble, but I found their anger easier to deal with than their hurt, so I ignored the voice.

When they came through the arrivals gate it was as if they'd brought a little bit of home with them. It was so good to hear them speak with their soft, Norfolk accents. For a moment I was transported to England; the sun was shining, the barley was golden and all was well with the world. Then I caught site of the overcast day, the dark clouds heavy in the sky and I was back in Alaska and far from home. It wasn't always like this here of course, a lot of the time was bright and clear, but the good days were interspersed with the bad and at this time of year the weather was usually pretty awful.

I didn't feel so far from home now though, not now that Mum and Dad were here. We all flew into one another's arms in the manner of people who are close and who have been separated. Mum and I cried, and when I looked at Dad I could see that his eyes were glistening too.

Eventually we managed to compose ourselves, words tripping over one another "Did you have a good flight?" "How are you?" "What time did you leave?" "How's England?" "It's so good to be here!" and nobody really listening to the answers, it was just so good to be talking to each other again.

We transferred their luggage to the car, still talking nineteen to the dozen, and set off for the Apollo. Mum sat in the back and Dad sat beside me, admiring the car, and passing comments on my driving – *good* comments for a change, like how impressed he was that I'd taken to driving on the "wrong" side of the road so easily, and how well I handled a large car. For once he never criticised my speed and I wondered how long the "good-to-see-you-I-won't-say-anything-to-upset-you mood would last. Still, I made the most of it.

I could see in the rear-view mirror that Mum had closed her eyes and guessed that she'd had to do most of the arrangements regarding their trip. She wouldn't have actually done Dad's packing for him, but she would have made sure his clothes were all washed and ironed ready and generally running around like the proverbial blue-arsed fly. No wonder she was tired now. I let her sleep and Dad and I chatted in low voices.

He gave me a brief run down on what was happening in the village and passed on some messages from friends back home. I told him about my job and about singing with Nat's band, carefully editing out things that would cause distress, like being attacked.

It was a little more than a half-hour trip to the Apollo. Once there I helped Mum and Dad up to the room with their luggage, parked the car in the hotel's park and said goodnight. Mum made a feeble protest about me leaving so soon but her heart wasn't really in it. I told them that I'd see them in the morning. Dad worried about me walking home alone in the dark but I pointed out that this was Alaska, not London, and I'd be perfectly safe, not that I necessarily believed what I said, of course. Besides, this time of year it was dark more than it was light and I'd hardly leave home at all if I'd only go out during daylight. That didn't mean that I didn't have my eyes peeled for possible attackers every time I was outside, but especially in the hours of darkness.

It was snowing when I left the flat the next morning. I was dressed in my normal winter going out clothes and they were so heavy I didn't dare take the elevator in the Apollo so I laboured up the stairs to my parent's room. This had the added bonus of postponing for a further few minutes this morning's confessions to Mum and Dad.

They both looked well rested. Mum was dancing up and down with excitement at the falling snow. She wasn't like me, she *loved* the snow.

I took off my outer clothes and threw them on the bed.

"Go down to the bar, shall we?" I suggested. I'd checked out the bar as I walked through the foyer and there weren't too many people in there so it would be comfortable chatting, but there were *some* people there, which meant that neither Mum nor Dad would make a scene – they were English, after all. And the bar would be more comfortable to sit in. Although the rooms were equipped with armchairs there were only two so one of us would have had to sit on the bed. Not that there was anything wrong with that but I planned to be there a while.

We trooped down the stairs – Mum wasn't fond of elevators – and she and I sat down while Dad went and ordered drinks before joining us.

"Now," Mum said, once we were all settled, "tell us everything you've been up to. I know you talked to Dad in the car but, well, I missed most of it," she smiled.

"I've told you most of it anyway," I said, "in all those emails and 'phone calls."

Dad picked up a newspaper and buried his nose in it. He wasn't interested in women's chatter. He'd seen me and satisfied himself that I was still standing and that I looked well and that was good enough for him.

"There must be loads more to day though," Mum protested, and waited, looking expectant.

"Well," I began, "I like my job; I've made some good friend's; I'm singing with Nat's band in the evenings –"

"Nat?" Mum questioned.

This was the moment then. Go for it, girl,

"Nat's one of the good friends I mentioned. He lives one side of my flat and another good friend, Cindy, lives on the other side." Best not to mention Cindy's profession.

Mum looked puzzled. "Flat? This is the new apartment you told me you'd moved to, is it? With Glen? Where is he, by the way, I thought that he'd put in an appearance at least?"

I smiled, but I could feel my lips trembling. "I'm not living with Glen any more," I blurted out. "We've split up and I've moved out and I'm living in the flat on my own." It all came out in a rush now.

"Oh!" Mum sat back in her chair.

Dad put the paper down.

"It's okay," I hurried on, "I'm really happy. The flat – sorry, apartment – is small but cosy and … and …" I faltered.

There was silence. I could hear the clock ticking at the other end of the bar. *Tick, tock, tick, tock.*

"Say something," I pleaded.

The silence continued and then Mum leant forward. "When you were seven we discovered you'd been awarded a gold star for English. *You* didn't tell us, we met your teacher in the street and *she* told us.

"When you were 15 you got the lead in the school play and the first we knew of it was when you brought the programme home and told us you'd got us a couple of tickets. Even then we had to read in the programme that you were going to be in it, *you* didn't tell us.

"When you decided to leave home and come halfway across the world the first indication that we had of what you were planning was when you put the airline tickets on the dining table."

She paused.

"And your point?" I asked, knowing exactly what her point was.

She sighed. "My point," she said, "Is that you never tell us anything soon enough. Everything's done and dusted by the time we find out."

"Are you saying," I asked, "that if I'd told you earlier you would have persuaded me not to leave Glen?"

She shook her head. "Of course not. I can't pretend that I'm sorry about that." She picked up her vodka and orange and took a huge gulp, coughed and resumed. "The point is you were over here all on your own, struggling with a break up and finding a new place to live. If you'd told us what was happening then we'd have suggested that you come home. You didn't give us the chance to be the loving, supportive parents that we want to be."

"Oh, Mum," I hugged her. "I knew that you were there for me if I needed you, and that's the main thing." I picked up my own drink. "The thing is," I settled back against the back of the sofa, "I didn't *want* to come home." No, that wasn't right. It didn't sound very kind and besides, it wasn't true, "That is," I continued hastily, "I would have loved to come home, of course I would. But I didn't want to come home and have everyone say that they told me so,"

"Do you think that we would have done that?" Mum looked pained.

"Well, maybe not in so many words, but the meaning would have been the same."

Dad made a noise that sounded like "hrmmph" and buried his head back in his paper. Dad wasn't good at emotion. His support lay in the practical area.

"So what happened then," Mum asked, "between you and Glen?"

"Actually, Mum, it was a lot worse than you think."

Dad's paper went down again and the blood drained from Mum's face.

"Did he hurt you?" Mum asked. "I'll kill him if he did." She looked as though she was about to get up and go and find Glen right now. I put a hand on her arm.

"No, Mum, he didn't hurt me – at least not physically."

"Well, what then? What could be worse?"

I looked down at my lap. "I don't know how to say this," I began, "but I've got no money left."

"What? But we gave you thousands," Mum was gobsmacked, as well she might be. "What have you done with it all?"

I looked up, meeting the shock in her eyes.

"Sorry," she said, "I didn't mean it to come out like that. I know that this is difficult for you and I don't want to make it any harder than it is already."

"That's all right, Mum. I know that this is a shock for you." I smiled a trembling smile. "Glen," I said, "Glen took everything. Oh mum, he cleaned out the bank account and sold everything that I'd bought for the home."

"But how could he? Why didn't you keep an eye on things? You *knew* what he was like; we told you. Why did you let him get away with it?"

Oh boy, this was turning out to be every bit as difficult as I expected. Mum was crying now. I knew that they were tears of frustration because I *hadn't* listened to their warnings about Glen. The tears that *I* was crying were for the same reason. How could I have been so stupid? How could I have let Mum and Dad down so badly?

Dad put out a hand and patted Mum's arm. "Leave it, Ginny, you're both upset now. We can talk about it later, when we've had time to think about it." He turned to me and smiled.

"I'm proud of you, princess. You made a mistake but you didn't come crying to us but you stood on your own two feet and sorted your life out. Well done. You've grown up."

I blinked back the tears and smiled gratefully.

"Thanks, Dad. The flat's not much but it's quite cosy now I've given it a lick of paint."

"I bet it is. You always did have the makings of a home-maker. When you were small there was nothing you liked better than doing a bit of housework."

Gosh, how times had changed. These days I was happy doing the bare minimum and it was one of the great things about living in a flat – there wasn't much to clean. The downside was that I had to put things away all the time otherwise it looked a mess in no time at all.

"And don't take any notice of your Mum," he continued. "She's tired and overwrought and just worried about you, princess. She loves you to bits, you know, we both do. But that doesn't mean that seeing you growing up and away from us is easy to get to grips with."

I nodded. "I know, Dad."

Mum took out some tissues and blew her nose and wiped her eyes and I did the same. We caught each other's eyes and she smiled a watery smile.

"Oh, I'm sorry, sweetheart," she said, "I shouldn't have had a go at you; you've obviously been through a lot and," she shrugged, "what's money when compared to your health and well-being. As long as you're all right, then that's the main thing."

"I will come home," I said, grateful that the worse seemed to be over, "of course I will, but I wanted to save enough to pay my own way."

"Of course you did. And how much have you saved so far?"

I looked down at my lap again. "One hundred and twenty dollars," I muttered.

"How much? I didn't hear."

I looked up. "A hundred and twenty dollars, Mum. I'm having to pay rent and buy food you know."

"It's all right," she said, "I'm not going to have a go at you, I just wondered how much difference our Christmas present would make."

"Huh?"

Mum looked at Dad and Dad looked back at Mum. Neither of them said anything and yet somehow I sensed that they had communicated.

"We'll be giving you money for Christmas," Mum said. "We didn't want to have to carry anything heavy because of the luggage limitations, and we thought that money would be useful for you." She grimaced. "Turns out we were right, but for the wrong reasons. So we're going to give you a cheque. Unfortunately it won't be enough to get you a ticket home but it will help towards it." She frowned, "As long as you don't spend it all."

"I won't Mum, honest." I got up and hugged her, then I hugged Dad. "Thank you, both of you, for being so understanding. I *am* coming home and it won't take me that long to save the rest of the fare. I've got another five months to run on my visa, so I've breathing space."

"Well, we can't wait to have you home, sweetheart. You come home and stay with us for a while until you sort out a job and somewhere to live?"

I looked at her, surprised.

"You can stay with us just as long as you want – forever, if you like, but you might not find it so easy living back with us now that you've tasted independence."

I realised that she was probably right, and wasn't she just great for seeing what might happen. Sometimes I thought she knew me better than I knew myself.

We spent the rest of the morning chatting, then after a meal in the hotel restaurant I returned the hire car and we walked back to my flat. Mum and Dad said that they loved the flat but I could sense their disappointment that I was stuck here for the time being and not winging my way home with them. Nonetheless they walked round admiring the curtains I'd made and the colours that I'd used to brighten the place up. They sat on the sofa and pronounced it comfortable, had a coffee drunk from my new mugs, and then later I walked back with them to their hotel and had a drink in the bar before leaving them.

When I got home there was a man watching my flat.

CHAPTER TEN

I called Nat once I'd got into the flat and bolted the door behind me.

"I can't see anyone, hun," Nat said when I told him about the watcher. "I'm looking out of the window now."

I crossed the room and peered down at the spot where the man had been standing. He'd gone.

I looked along the street.

"There, Nat," I shouted, pointing as though Nat was in the room with me, "just going past the draper's."

"Okay, I see him," Nat said, "and if you shout any louder you can do away with the 'phone and just call through the wall."

"Oh, sorry. But you *do* see him?"

"Yes, hun, I do. How do you know that he was watching your flat?"

"Well, he just *was.*"

Actually, how *did* I know? He'd certainly been standing on the opposite side of the road and looking at the building and he *could* have been looking directly at the windows to my flat, but equally he could have been looking at Cindy's or Nat's windows or even the floor above or below me. I hadn't been close enough to him to see exactly where his gaze had settled.

"You don't think you might be getting a little paranoid, Laura, do you?"

"Hell, no, Nat. I've had my apartment broken into and turned over and I've come close to being assaulted. I think I'm entitled to be a bit concerned if I think there's someone got his eye on my flat, don't you?" My voice had risen, both in decibels and tone.

"Sorry, you're right of course. Want me to come round?"

"No, you're all right, Nat, thanks." My voice was calmer now. "I'm okay." I shut the 'phone and pulled the curtains across the windows. Not that anyone could see in, it wasn't as though I was on the ground floor, but I just felt safer somehow if the world was shut out.

I got changed into my pyjamas and climbed into bed where I lay awake, tossing and turning and listening for sounds of someone on the stairs. I knew that the residents were more careful these days about closing the front door but I knew, too, that it would be easy for an intruder to slip in with a resident as they entered. If they looked confident enough about their right to be there I didn't think there were too many people who would question them. Alaskan people were friendly but not intrusive, and they tended to keep their noses out of other people's business.

Eventually, realising that I *wasn't* about to wrap myself in the arms of slumber I got up and put the light on. It was three days to Christmas and I still had presents to wrap so for the next couple of hours I occupied myself with presents, scissors, wrapping paper and sealing tape.

Wrapping gifts doesn't use too much brainpower and my mind wandered back across the past year. This time last year I'd been at home, doing something similar. If someone had told me then that in a year's time I would be living in Alaska I would have told them not to talk rubbish. I'd lived in the same small Norfolk town all my life and if I imagined a future at all it never included crossing an ocean.

I'd grown up a lot in the past year, and I wondered if Mum and Dad noticed or if I'd always, to them, be their "little girl".

I thought about Glen; how it had been love at first sight. He'd been staying with a relative in Norwich and had borrowed his aunt's car in which he was touring the county. He'd stopped in at the newsagents in the village and was coming out as I was going in. Something about me must have appealed because he was waiting for me when I came out clutching my local paper and a bar of chocolate. Maybe he just knew that I was stupid and gullible,

I thought the long hair and torn clothes that he wore were cool. We didn't get many rebels in our village and maybe it was his very difference that attracted me. Oh, and he could make a guitar sing like I'd never heard before, but of course I didn't find that out until later.

Nor did I find out about his habit and the lengths that he would go to to support it until much later. His parents had paid for his trip to England in the hope that getting him away from the crowd that he ran with back home would cure him. They weren't very "up" in drug know-how or maybe they didn't realise how heavily Glen was addicted. Anyway, I'm sure that they didn't realise that it would take only hours in a new country for their son to set up his contacts. I discovered later that he stole from his aunt and uncle while he was with them, not just money but other things that he found hidden away and that he guessed they wouldn't miss until he was long gone. A week before he left he took a painting that was hanging in his bedroom to the local art room and got £500 for it.

I didn't know this then, of course, or I would never have followed him to America. At least I *hope* that I wouldn't. You can't know though, can you? Had I been so besotted by him that I would have followed him to the ends of the earth? Was it only when his selfishness affected me personally that the veils were drawn from my eyes and I could see him for what he really was?

I was done with him now though, and that was the main thing. For the first few weeks after I left I was worried that I might bump into him. He only lived across town, less than four miles away from me. But he wasn't likely to be in the places where I went – work, clubs, shops. He would be in the *dark* side of town, down the alleys, among the refuse bins, where the streets stank of urine and rotting vegetables.

I shuddered now, just thinking of him, remembering him running his hands over my flesh.

Yes, I thought, I was certainly done with him now. The mere thought of him made me shudder. I'd learnt a few things about myself in this past year as well, and about human nature in general.

At 2.30 I pulled back the curtains. "Just checking", I told myself. But the street was empty. I climbed back into bed and was asleep within minutes.

Next day I had to go to work. I'd got some days off after Christmas that I would spend with Mum and Dad. I knew that today they were looking forward to exploring the local shops and were going to call in on Con. I'd told him they were coming and he was planning on having us all over one evening after Christmas. An evening spent with Con – what could be more delightful? Actually, an evening spent in a morgue would come close in the fun stakes.

After work I'd agreed to go to the Apollo and have dinner with Mum and Dad but I went home to change first. As I turned the corner into my street I could see that the same man that had been there the day before was standing watching the flat again. I pulled out my cell 'phone and called Nat.

"He's there again, Nat," I said when Nat answered. "Watching the flat."

"Hang on," Nat said, "Oh yes. He's not looking up at the flats though."

"No," I said, "He's looking at me. Uh-oh, He's crossed over and he's coming my way."

"Keep walking," Nat said, "and keep talking. I'm on my way down."

The man, like most Alaskan inhabitants at this time of year, was swathed in gloves and scarves, so it was impossible to get a good look at him, but he was about the same height and build as one of the guys who'd attacked me after the gig. He'd got his head down anyway, so I couldn't see his face.

He was level with me now and looked as though he was going to walk right past.

Next thing I knew I was on the floor, face down on the ice. In front of me were two black boots. My assailant yanked my arm up and tore off my gloves (I was wearing two pairs). I tried to raise my head and saw the door to the apartment building fly open and Nat's trainers come up behind my attacker.

Suddenly a body fell on top of me. My chin cracked on the ice and all the air left my body.

"Sorry, hun. Hang on." Nat managed to pull the man off of me and he grabbed me under my arms and pulled me to my feet. There was a moment when we began to slide precariously and I thought that we were going to land in a jumbled heap on top of my attacker, but, using his body, we managed to get some purchase. Eventually I stood upright, cradled in Nat's arms.

"You okay, Laura?" Nat's eyes were full of concern. He ran a finger across my chin. "Gonna have another beauty of a bruise there. Come on, let's get you inside and then I'll call the cops."

I was still dazed. "What happened, Nat? What did you do?"

"I karate chopped him," Nat said proudly, "I've been taking lessons"

"But … but when we thought there might be somebody in my flat – " my voice faltered. How could I say 'you went and got Cindy' which would make him sound cowardly, when it was he who had just saved me from the attacker.

Carefully, he guided me towards the outer door of the apartment block. Behind me I could hear groaning, but I didn't dare turn round to see if my attacker was getting back on his feet. I tried to hurry though, in case he was.

"I passed the buck," Nat admitted, in response to my incomplete question. "Although I had thought that the three of us – mob handed, might be more of a match for an intruder. I didn't *know* that Cindy would march in on her own." He looked thoughtful. "I guess I should have known that's what she'd do though. She's little but she's got bottle." He grinned at me. "Anyway, I decided I needed to hone up my defensive skills so I've been taking martial arts classes. I've only had a couple, but apparently I'm a natural, or so I'm told."

"Well, good for you, Nat," I said "And thank God you were here today."

"Never mind that. I'm just glad you're okay."

We reached the steps to the apartment building and Nat helped me up them and into the lobby. There was a seat there and he gently lowered me into it; I didn't seem to be able to function by myself at the moment.

"I'll be back in a second," he said and I watched him go out of the building, stand outside and look up and down the street. I could see the amazement on his face. He turned and faced me.

"He's gone, Laura," he said. "The bastard's gone."

I leaned back in my chair and sighed. The git had gone because Nat had been more concerned about me than apprehending my attacker. I couldn't blame him for that. And I don't know what Nat would have done if the guy had still been there. I was very grateful to Nat, but I couldn't help but think he'd struck lucky and taken my assailant by surprise. If he'd gone back for another try he might not have been so lucky.

But what was going on? Why had I been attacked? Was this guy still looking for Russ? And why pick on *me?* *I* didn't know where Russ was, for God's sake. Surely they realised that by now?

Nat handed me his 'phone. "I've dialled the cops," he said, "all you've got to do is tell them what happened."

I shut off the connection and shook my head.

"What's the point, Nat?" I said, resignation in my voice. "I can't even describe the guy, he was too well wrapped up for that."

"Laura," Nat said sternly, "this is the second time you've been physically attacked. Next time you might be on your own. Ring the police."

"I'll ring them tomorrow," I promised.

"Didn't you get a severe telling off last time you delayed it until the next day?"

I nodded. "Maybe so, but right now," I struggled to get out of the chair, "I've got to go and get changed and get myself round to the Apollo for dinner with Mum and Dad."

"Oh, Laura, you are the limit." Nat stepped forward and put a supporting arm under my elbow. "Come on then. When you're ready give me a knock and I'll walk you round to the Apollo."

I smiled at him gratefully. "Thanks, Nat."

An hour later I presented myself at his door. I'd applied a lot of foundation again to try and hide the bruise but I think that I was going to have to admit to Mum and Dad that I'd fallen over. There was no need for them to know the circumstances of the fall.

"You know, I've been thinking," I said to Nat as we walked arm in arm towards the Apollo. "I don't think that this *was* one of the guys that attacked me outside the night-club."

"Oh?"

"The guys that night kept asking me where Russ was. The brute tonight didn't say a word, he just yanked my arm up."

"So why do you think that he attacked you?"

I pulled off my gloves and waved my hand in front of his face. "My rings," I said, hurriedly replacing the glove. "They're valuable. Especially the one with the rubies," I explained. "My grandparents gave it to my Mum on her twenty-first birthday. They had quite a bit of money then, although they lost most of it later. Mum gave it to me as a leaving home present. It's worth about ... I don't know ... probably about 1000 dollars. Not a fortune, of course, but a tidy sum. And the other ring my parents gave me on my 18th birthday. I don't know how much that one cost, but it was probably a fair amount."

Nat whistled. "Wow. But how would he know? I mean even if he'd been watching you he wouldn't have been able to see your hands because you always wear gloves when you're out."

"True, but I don't indoors. Not in the flat, I don't mean, but – well, take tonight for instance. I'll be in public in the dining room at the hotel, *and* in the bar. And at work. I don't wear gloves at work." I frowned. "Now I come to think about it, I don't think it's any of those places anyway. The guy would have to know his jewellery to know that it's valuable *and* would have had to have had a close up view of it. Plus there's plenty of women wear more valuable jewellery than I do. No, I don't think it's any of those things."

"What then?"

I thought for a moment.

"Glen," I said quietly.

"Glen? Surely not. Why?"

"Think about it, Nat. 1000 dollars would buy quite a lot of smack, or coke or acid, or whatever Glen's drug of choice is at the moment. He wouldn't come himself, of course, I'd recognise him and run a mile, but it would be easy enough for him to find out where I was living and get one of his low-life mates to steal the ring."

"Wouldn't it be a bit of a gamble though? You might not be wearing the ring."

"Glen knows that I *always* wear the ring. The only time that I take it off is when I'm in the bath or washing up, otherwise it's right there on my finger. I'm *sure* that Glen is behind this latest escapade."

"Hmm. You could be right. I think that's even more reason for you to call the cops."

"I will, Nat, I promise. Tomorrow." We were at the Apollo now. "Coming in for a drink – meet my parents?"

Nat shook his head. "Another time maybe. If I come in with you now you'll only be worrying about what your Mum and Dad think of me and are they imagining that we're an item, and how do you tell them we're not without offending me – and all that. No, I think you need to relax. But if your Dad doesn't walk you home then you make sure that you call me and I'll be here. I've not got a gig tonight."

"No hot date?" I smiled up at him.

He grinned. "No, that's tomorrow. So promise you won't walk home alone?"

I nodded. "Promise."

He kissed my nose. "Go on, enjoy. See you later."

I stopped at the door and waved to Nat before entering the warmth and luxury of the Apollo.

CHAPTER ELEVEN

Mum and Dad were sitting on one of the leather sofas in the foyer when I entered the Apollo. Dad was reading the paper and Mum a book. Mum looked up and smiled when she saw me, putting her book to one side. As I got closer though, her smile changed to a look of horror. Damn! I obviously hadn't covered the bruise as well as I thought. Maybe this bruise, coming so soon after the one I'd received the night of the attack after the gig, was never going to be disguisable.

"I'm okay," I said, before Mum could ask any awkward questions. "I fell. Silly really," I went on, "I should be used to the sidewalks being slippery, but I slipped over on my way home from work tonight. Now tell me," I sat between them on the sofa, "what have you two been doing today."

After some discussion about *how* I'd fell, *where* I'd fell and what had I put on the injury to try and stop it hurting they eventually proceeded to regale me with tales of their exploration of the town.

"That Con's not how I remember him," Mum said. "He was a nice little boy when I last saw him."

"That was about 25 years ago Mum. What was he then, about 10?"

"Well, yes," Mum admitted, "but he was so slim in those days."

Yeah, I thought, and now he's slug-fat with a bald head and –

"Did you buy anything nice?" I asked, shutting off thoughts of Con.

Mum shook her head and Dad buried his head in the paper again. Shopping wasn't really his scene. He must have hated being dragged round the shops today. Although maybe not; Dad liked new places and would have been looking at the architecture and exploring alley-ways while Mum fingered the linens and admired the china in the shops.

Mum shook her head. "We didn't, no. To be honest we don't have that much room on our baggage allowance. We will take some souvenirs back with us, but I'll leave it until a few days before we go home.

Go home. They'd only just arrived; I couldn't bear the thought of them flying back to England and leaving me here.

I gave myself a mental shake. This was ridiculous. Sure, I was homesick and I guess it was worse in a way now that Mum and Dad were here, somehow it reminded me of all that I was missing. But for now I must just enjoy having them here, and when they did finally go then I'd remind myself that we wouldn't be parted for ever; I'd be going home in the not-too-distant future.

69

And I wasn't unaware that my returning home would mean that I'd be leaving good friends behind. It seemed that in future, wherever I was then I'd be missing someone! What a crazy life.

Dinner at the Apollo was excellent. I'd heard it was but had never been able to afford to sample more than the tea that Maisie and I had enjoyed. Meals weren't over-the-top expensive, but they weren't cheap either, even in the Sun room, which was the less expensive of the two restaurants in the hotel and the one open to the public – the Artemis being confined to guests at the hotel and *their* guests.

After dinner, by which time we all declared that we were full to bursting point, we went and sat in the lounge.

"Only two days to Christmas," Mum said, gazing round her at the festive decorations. I had to admit that the Apollo had pulled out all the stops when it came to decorating the place. There was a huge tree just inside the front door that only fitted because the ceilings were about twelve foot high. There were other, smaller trees dotted about the place and garlands festooned the ceilings. Soft Christmas music played in the background, a mixture of modern, traditional and classical. The air smelt of cranberries and wood-smoke and I found myself remembering Christmas' past and wondering what future Christmases would hold for me.

"We've booked you in here for the Christmas dinner, of course," mum told me as we relaxed with a coffee following the meal – full strength, almost black, brazenly bitter coffee.

"Lovely," I said, although in truth I hadn't considered the logistics of the day. Now I did. "You'll come to me for the present-opening-ceremony, won't you?" I asked, mentally ticking off in my head that I'd got enough cups/seats/drinking glasses.

"Of course we will, love."

The present-opening-ceremony was traditionally held after breakfast in our house. Everyone had to be washed and dressed, there was never any peeking beforehand, although when I was very young I'd been allowed to open one small present the night before, but that had stopped when I reached my teens.

I'd been looking at the decorations but I looked back at Mum just in time to see her frown at dad. *Zip it,* the frown said, *the flat is our daughter's home and if she wants us to go there then we* will.

Yeah, Dad would naturally prefer to stay in the warmth and luxury of the Apollo rather than venture out in the cold and slum it in my flat. If he thought about it there's no way that he'd say that though, he was sensitive enough to know that would hurt my feelings. The trouble was that Dad's motto was "speak first, think later", and this meant that Mum's main role in life was to guestimate what Dad was about to say at any given moment and warn him off if she thought that it was going to be inappropriate. I'd got used to the silent language between my parents and could usually work out what was going on between the two of them. I envied them that knowledge of each other and wondered if I would ever share that level of intimacy with someone.

I had, at least, got a few decorations up in the flat. The office had shelled out for new ones to decorate my place of work and the old ones had been offered to the staff. Few of us wanted them, most of us having already built up our own suitcases full of items only used in the festive season, which meant that I was able to grab for myself more than enough to decorate my little flat. I'd even got one of those optic Christmas trees, but turned it on sparingly, ever mindful of the electricity it was using, not only for my bank balance's sake but also with the environment in mind. It was the only "plus" side for not having a computer; it meant that I was saving on electricity and helping the environment by not printing off every damn thing I looked at on screen. I was seriously considering not getting a printer at all when I finally purchased a computer; that would certainly save on paper.

"Good," I said now, glad that they hadn't suggested coming to me for lunch! Rightly or wrongly I had assumed that we'd all be eating our Christmas Dinner together at the hotel. If they had overlooked making that arrangement then I would have ended up eating muffins alone in my flat for Christmas dinner.

"Con said," Mum went on, "that you were in a bit of a state when he took you to see the flat."

I looked at her. What else had Con told her? Not, I hoped about the break-ins at the flat; that would worry her to death. But no, she looked puzzled rather than overly concerned. "He said," she continued, "that he took pity on you so rushed everything through quickly so you could move into the flat straight away. The thing is," she stirred her coffee thoughtfully, "he doesn't strike me as a man who would do anything unless it suited him and if he was getting something out of it."

"Mum!" Surely she wasn't suggesting what I thought she might be suggesting? That Con had done me a favour in exchange for favours returned?

"What?"

"For a start Con didn't do me any favours. The guy who had the flat before me did a runner and left owing Con several week's rent. Con couldn't wait to get somebody else installed in the apartment and paying rent and I just happened along at the right time. He charges me the same rent as anyone else and I don't even have a contract. Con's done nobody any favours except himself." I just stopped myself in time pointing out that he hadn't even got me decent furniture to replace the awful stuff that had been damaged in the break in.

Mum looked relieved, as well she might. "That's all right, then. Fancy not giving you a reduction on the rent though. You are family, after all."

"Yes, but it's a fact I would rather not be reminded of, thank you, not when it comes to Con."

Mum laughed. Dad muttered something under his breath that sounded like "He's no relative of mine, thank God," and I guessed they had as little respect for Con as did I.

We were sitting in the lounge and it was very peaceful. I was full of good food, had the people I most loved in the world with me, it was warm and the air was sweet, I felt myself drifting off.....

When I woke up, Dad had disappeared and Mum was beside me, her eyes closed. I looked at the clock, it was twenty past nine and I'd been asleep for over half an hour.

Reluctantly, I pulled myself up from the slouching position I'd fallen into while asleep. Mum's eyes opened.

"Was I asleep?" she asked unnecessarily.

"You were," I told her, "but so was I."

Dad appeared at that moment. "Ah, my sleeping beauties both awake now, are they?"

I stretched. "Time for me to be wending my merry way, I think, and letting you two get to bed."

"I'll walk you home," Dad said, turning on his heel, "I'll just get my coat."

"I'll come with you," Mum said, " the cold air will wake me up."

They both hurried off to the stairs to go to their room and I relaxed. Might as well enjoy the luxury for a minute or two longer. I glanced out into the foyer and noticed a man sitting in one of the armchairs reading a paper. As I watched he lowered his newspaper and looked straight at me.

I gasped. It was scar-face, one of the goons from the incident in the alley the night I was with the band. My blood suddenly turned icy cold.

72

The guy stood up and disappeared through the revolving doors before I'd gathered my thoughts enough to think straight. Then my first thought was for my parents. Had I put them in danger by coming here? By being seen in their company? Would the goons now turn their attention to Mum and Dad, thinking that *they* might know where Russ was?

What should I do? Should I warn them they might be in danger? But then they'd worry about me and the danger *I* might be in. Crap! Why was life so complicated? My life, anyway.

I couldn't, I just couldn't, tell them. That would lead to explanations about break-ins and attacks and all sorts of things I didn't want them to know about.

I smiled at them when they came down, wrapped up well in their coats, mufflers and gloves, mum with her fur-lined boots and Dad with something that looked very much like wellies on his feet. I hoped my smile reached my eyes and didn't show the trepidation I was feeling inside; I knew mum could read me like an open book and kept my eyes from meeting hers for fear she'd read the worry written there.

"We wondered if your friend, Sara, might like to join us for dinner tomorrow or on Christmas Eve," Mum said as we walked the icy streets. "Or maybe Cindy or Nat?"

"Or all three, if they wanted," Dad added.

"We'd like to get to know them, you see," Mum said, "so that when we're back home we can imagine you with your friends and what you'll be doing."

You have no idea, mum, what could be happening, judging by recent events. And it's best that it stays that way.

"Besides," Mum continued, "you've told us such a lot about them; they're obviously all important to you."

I squeezed her arm. "Not as important as you and Dad though, Mum, but yes, they're all important in their own way. I thought of Cindy, so strong and fearless, and such a contradiction in terms with her pole-dancing and her girl-next-door look. I thought of Nat, a lot of people would call him a layabout, but I knew he worked hard with the band, it was he who kept them together, who made sure they rehearsed regularly, organised gigs and generally kept them on the straight and narrow. Plus I knew, which a lot of people didn't, that he was a songwriter of some note. When he got back from gigs he'd sit into the early hours writing new songs, some of which had been recorded by some top artists, and one of which was even now storming its way into the hit parade.

73

Then there was Sara. She and I had hit it off from the word go. We'd only seen each other a few times since we first met, yet she'd fallen easily into the "best friend" slot. But in reality I knew very little about her. I knew she'd been involved with Russ, of course, and that Tommy was Russ' son. I knew her father had run his own business and was now semi-retired and that they were happy keeping Sara and little Tommy until she got her life sorted out. But I didn't actually know what job Sara had done before becoming a mum, or what music she liked, or what other boyfriends she had. So far all our conversations had been about Russ and his disappearance or my Mum and Dad's impending arrival. Oh, and we'd touched on the little things in life, inconsequential chatter that friends exchange, which means nothing but eases the friendship along.

When they left me at the door to the apartment block I felt as though I should follow Mum and Dad back to the hotel, just to make sure that nobody was following them and intending them harm. Instead, I kissed them goodnight and let myself into the apartment block, carefully closing the door behind me.

I went up the stairs slowly, my mind in a whirl. I had no more idea what was happening than I had after the first break in. Everyone seemed to be looking for Russ, or for something they thought he had. For some reason the goons thought I might know something. I racked my brain – was it possible I'd picked up something from the previous tenant without realising its importance and either thrown it away or still had it?

No, I decided, there was nothing that fit that bill. Whatever they were looking for had either disappeared with Russ or was still in the flat.

I unlocked the apartment door and let myself in.

CHAPTER TWELVE

There had been no warning that anything out of the ordinary was about to happen. My apartment door was closed tightly and I'd had to unlock it to get in. There were no wet footprints on the floor that would have indicated somebody else had made their way in through snow-clad pavements and dripped melting snow up the stairs and across the landing. So the stranger on my sofa came as a complete surprise.

He spun round when I opened the door and, to be honest, he looked as scared as I felt. I didn't see it at the time though; all I saw was an intruder in my flat.

My first instinct was to run – to go and get Nat, or maybe Cindy - she had, after all, proved herself the bravest of the three of us the last time my flat had been violated. But hey, this was my home; it may not be much, but it was all that I had got and I didn't take kindly to strangers wandering in when they pleased. I decided to stay and stand my ground.

That all went through my mind in a split second. I opened my mouth to suggest that the guy leave the way he came and to make it snappy when he jumped up. "It's okay," he said, "please don't scream". He rushed past me and slammed the door shut. I spun round, horrified. I hadn't been very clever there, had I? Now I was trapped in my own flat with a possible marauding mass-murderer. Although, as I looked closer at him, I could see that my visitor looked less like a mass murderer and more like a startled mouse.

"I used to live here," he said. My name's –"

"Russ Bracken," I finished for him, wondering why I hadn't changed the locks when I moved in. How stupid was that?

I dumped my bags on the floor, put my hands on my hips and glared at him. "And what, may I ask, are you doing here? You don't live here any longer, you know, and I think you have one or two responsibilities that should be pressing on you and ensuring that you don't spend time dilly-dallying in the homes of people you don't know. It's time that you cleared up the mess that you left behind you so that innocent people could get a decent night's sleep!" Anger was taking over the fear I felt and I was damn well going to let him know that I couldn't be walked over any more.

He stared at me, open mouthed, as though I had no right to have a go at him. Or maybe he was as surprised as I was that I'd dare.

"And I suggest," I said, pulling my cell phone from my bag, "that you leave right now before I call the cops."

He had the phone out of my hand in a heartbeat. Uh-oh, I'd been stupid again.

I looked behind me and tried to work out whether I could get to the closed door before he did, but before I could make a move he spoke again.

"I'm not going to hurt you, honestly," he said, "but we can't have the cops here and I can't risk you calling anybody else."

"So you're going to keep my phone?" I asked, aghast. All my contact numbers were in there, many of which I didn't know off by heart.

He nodded. "Until you hear me out," he said, "then you can have it back and call whoever you want to."

I looked at him earnestly. He really didn't look like much of a threat. I was quite tall and he stood only about a few centimetres taller. His reddish hair and pale skin made him look quite delicate, and I decided that, if it came to it, I could probably do as much damage to him as he could to me. He didn't look like a fighter.

I sighed, "Okay, you can have ten minutes." I seated myself on one of the stools at the breakfast bar. "Spill."

He perched back down on the edge of the sofa and took a deep breath. "As you know, my name is Russ Bracken. I work for Alusa Stationery on Fifth Avenue. My job involves my travelling round the country – or it did, I'm not sure at the moment whether I'm still employed by the company. Anyway," he brushed a hand through his thinning hair, "I'm also a bit of an amateur photographer, get lots of good pictures as I travel round, especially in the snow."

"Which there's a lot of," I added, dryly.

"Which there's a lot of," he agreed. "Anyway, most of my pictures are scenes – you know, snow clad mountains, trees dripping with ice, that kind of thing. Sometimes there are people in my photographs, they provide a human interest, and sometimes," here he paused for effect, "sometimes the people that turn up in the pictures turn out to be people being where they're not supposed to be."

"Oh?" I was getting bored and wondered where this was leading.

"And sometimes," he continued, "those people have an alibi for the time the photograph was taken and their alibi says that they were somewhere else completely."

"Oh?" My vocabulary, of which I was normally quite proud, seemed to have deserted me, but at least my interest was piqued.

Russ Bracken leant forward on the sofa and met my eyes. "And sometimes having photos that put those people in the wrong place at the wrong time can prove to be quite dangerous."

"Oh," There I go again. Next time I'm going to say "Really?" just by way of a change.

"Heard of Carl Demain?" Russ asked.

You bet I had! I think most people in Alaska had heard of Carl Demain, even newcomers like me. When I first arrived here the media had carried stories of Carl Demain and his possible involvement in a kidnapping case. From what I could recall he had a watertight alibi for the time of the crime, putting him far away from the house from which a toddler had been taken.

The kidnapping had occurred somewhere Anchorage way as far as I could recall, and Carl Demain was apparently playing poker with several of his buddies at the time in a small town some two hundred miles away from Anchorage.

Demain was an entrepreneur in a bad way, with fingers in various pies. He'd served time when he was a young man for some kind of fraud crime, and when he came out of prison had set up on his own, buying and selling in a small way, all seemingly innocent and above board. By hook or by crook his merchant empire had grown and he now owned a chain of retail shops throughout Alaska, as well as companies which had developed some major software items and computer games.

The general census of opinion was that Demain had called in some overdue favours when he'd been accused of the kidnapping. Favours that resulted in getting him off of that particular hook.

He had, if my memory served me correctly, lost quite a bit of money in a lawsuit shortly before I arrived in Alaska. He had been sued by another computer company for stealing some ideas or blueprints or something. The exact details were hazy, but the child that had been kidnapped – and held for ransom – had been the offspring of the director of the company to which Demain had been required to pay vast sums of money in settlement. I couldn't remember all the details, but the child had been returned, traumatised but unhurt physically, but not before her parents had handed over vast amounts of money, probably about the same amount that Demain had needed to cough up to them following the court case.

It all seemed so obvious to an outsider. Demain had been ordered by the court to pay money to a second party and then the second party had handed over almost the exact amount to get his beloved child back from kidnappers. No wonder the police suspected Demain. But Demain had never been formally charged because of his alibi.

All this went through my brain in seconds, and on another level I was still trying to work out whether Russ Bracken could be trusted. Nat and Cindy hadn't really known him well enough to form an opinion, but Sara loved him and thought he was the bees-knees; surely she wouldn't have fallen for a guy who would harm me?

I kept myself alert, ready to run for the door or scream for help at the slightest sign of Russ turning nasty, but I nodded. "I've heard of him, yeah." See, my vocabulary was improving.

"Well, I've got a picture of Carl Demain taken on the day of the abduction that puts him right in the heart of Anchorage.

"What? So he *could* have done the kidnapping."

Russ nodded. "Sure could. And I have the proof."

"So let me get this straight. You, quite by accident, took a picture of Carl Demain in Anchorage at a time when he, and his mates, say he was miles away?"

"In Homer, that's right. And while I did take the picture by accident I did vaguely recognise Demain, and once the story about the kidnapping broke I was certain."

"Didn't you tell the police?"

"Of *course* I told the police. And that's why I'm in the mess I'm in."

"Oh?" I was off again on my perfectly formed sentences.

"I told the police as soon as I could, but Demain had already said that he had an alibi. But I knew that alibi was false. I wasn't travelling at the time so it was the local cops I told. That night two goons came to the flat, knocked me down and made off with my camera."

"Oh!"

"That made me a bit suspicious. So I let the police know that I'd had the camera stolen but told them that it was okay as I'd printed off a copy of the picture. I didn't come home though, and that night they broke into the flat again."

That must be the night that Cindy and Nat had told me about, the one where the door was broken down.

"And had you? Made a copy, I mean?"

"I've got several printed copies of the picture in various places, and several discs with copies of it on."

"But they won't be able to use them in court, will they?"

"Probably not, but if I can get copies to the right people then it'll make them dig a bit deeper and re-open the investigation into Demain's whereabouts that night."

"Hang on," it had just dawned on me what Russ had implied, "are you saying that the police are in on it?"

Russ shrugged. "I'm not saying anything really. But having my camera stolen on the night I tell them that I have a picture on it which implicates Demain did make me a mite suspicious."

"And then you told them you'd got copies," I said slowly, as I pieced the jigsaw together, "and the flat got broken into."

"That's right," Russ agreed, "and no matter how you look at it, it does seem to point a finger at the local cops."

I nodded agreement.

"I'm not saying," Russ continued, "that all the local cops are crooks. I don't think that for a minute. But someone is trying to protect Demain and I don't know who."

Other pieces of the jigsaw were falling into place. This could explain the break in since I'd lived here, and also the attack on my person by people unknown whose sole reason for living seemed to be to track down Russ Bracken. I knew now why they'd been so keen to know where he was.

"So what's your next step?" I asked.

He shrugged again. "I have absolutely no idea. The only reason I came back here is because I wanted to see if they were still looking for me and I thought that whoever was in the apartment might know." He glanced around him. "You've done a good job, by the way. Place looks really cheerful"

"Thanks." I was strangely gratified although anything done to the flat since Russ left would have had to have made an improvement.

I was trying to keep up with the developments in the bizarre conversation I was having while something unrelated kept tugging at my brain.

"What about Sara?" I asked suddenly.

"Sara?" He looked puzzled; as well he might at this abrupt change of subject. I, too, wanted to return to the subject of Carl Demain and tell Russ that yes, there were people still looking for him, but I needed to get this out of the way first, if only to reassure myself that Russ Bracken was, in fact, one of the good guys.

"Sara." I said patiently, "your fiancée, and little Tommy, your baby."

Russ looked puzzled. "I'm sorry, I don't know what you're talking about. I don't think I know anybody called Sara, and the only Tommy I know is Tommy Hilfiger. I do have a fiancée though," his face softened, "and her name is Siobhan. She's absolutely gorgeous."

"Hang on, hang on," I was trying to sort this out in my brain. "So who's Sara then?"

He frowned. "I told you, I don't know. I don't think I've *ever* known anyone called Sara. Oh, hang on, my grandmother's sister's name was Sara." He shook his head, "but she's been dead over twenty years."

"No," I said, "*My* – or rather *your* – Sara is about eighteen or nineteen, and Tommy is just a few weeks old." I put my head on one side and regarded Russ carefully. "Actually your son doesn't look a bit like you."

"He's not my son! As far as I know I don't have any children anywhere."

"So perhaps ...." I began, but I stopped. I was going to say that perhaps he'd not known Sara was pregnant, but Russ said he didn't know Sara and Sara herself had told me that she that Russ *had* known she was pregnant and that she'd seen him since Tommy was born.

"But Sara's been here. I've spent time with her and her family. They all maintain that you and Sara are getting married."

Russ's frown deepened. "That's not possible," he said, "I've only just got divorced and I'm planning on marrying Siobhan sometime next year, and then she and I and her son will be getting a place together."

Curiouser and curiouser, as Alice in Wonderland would say. Or maybe it wasn't her, but another character in her story.

"So who's Sara then?" I asked, sticking to reality.

"I have absolutely no idea. I've never heard of her and, to the best of my knowledge, never met her. And I've certainly never slept with anyone called Sara."

I stared at him, aghast at what he was implying.

Somebody was doing some serious lying, but who was it?

CHAPTER THIRTEEN

"Okay, so you don't know Sara. Or little Tommy. But why would Sara say you did?" I asked.

"I have absolutely no idea. But I have to assume that it's something to do with Demain. You say you met her father? What was he like?"

"I met her father *and* her mother," I told him, "and they were very nice people. The whole family's very nice. They made me feel very welcome and I've seen Sara and little Tommy several times. I'm seeing them tomorrow or Christmas Eve if they can make it. My parents are staying at-" I hesitated, I still didn't know if Russ was a good guy or one of the baddies; "-nearby," I finished, "and I'm hoping Sara and Tommy will come to dinner with them."

"Don't tell them you've seen me," Russ said, a note of panic creeping into his voice.

"Why not?" I asked. Gosh, I was thick sometimes.

"If they're telling you that she and I are an item then it's a lie," Russ said, "and the only reason for a lie like that is because she wants to find out if you've seen me. She's cultivated your friendship and cooked up this cock-and-bull story so that you'll tell her if anything happens to you that involves me."

I couldn't believe it.

"So who is she then?"

"I have absolutely no idea." Russ was beginning to overuse that phrase in my opinion, but I let it go. This time.

"I can only assume," he continued, "that she is somehow involved with Carl Demain and is using you to find me."

I still couldn't believe it. I couldn't believe that Sara could be involved with a crook like Demain, and I couldn't believe that she'd involve a baby in such a subterfuge. Besides, she'd seemed really nice, and I couldn't believe that I'd been taken in so badly and been so mistaken about anybody.

Then I remembered Sam.

Sam had been one of the most popular girls in my year at school. She had no time for me because I wasn't one of her sycophants, who were always running around after her, telling her how glamorous she looked and generally only existing to make her feel good about herself.

It wasn't just me, of course, half the class felt the same and the other half were her slaves. That was just the girls, of course. Pretty much *all* the boys only felt that they existed to serve her.

Then suddenly she started taking an interest in me. I can't deny that I was flattered that the most popular girl in the school wanted to be my friend and I was too innocent to realise that it might not be me she was interested in.

I was going out with Joe at the time. Joseph Morton, a really good-looking boy who I absolutely adored. Then before long I found that Sam was coming on nearly as many of our dates as I was. It started off with the flicks. I don't remember which film it was but whatever it was it was one that Sam had wanted to see for ages. "Can I come?" she'd asked eagerly. "Pleeeease," she'd begged, drawing out the word plaintively. "I wont get in the way, honest. You won't even know I'm there."

Joe had seemed a bit put out at first when he turned up to pick me up and found he had two passengers instead of one. He was working at the local garage so he was the only one of the three of us actually earning a wage, so he insisted on paying for Sara even though she made some token resistance.

I had imagined that Sara would sit beside me in the pictures, but actually she sat beside Joe. Then she chatted to him all through the film. As I said, I don't remember what the film was, but it was Notting Hill, or Love Actually, one of those chick-flicks that were so popular a few years ago. Not Joe's cup of tea at all, but he'd gallantly offered to take me when I said I'd like to see the film. But hadn't Sam said she'd like to see it as well? So why was she nattering all through it?

When Joe took me home we usually detoured down to the promenade and had a bit of a cuddle. Naturally that wasn't going to happen with Sam in the car, so my parents were pleasantly surprised by my early arrival home. At the door Joe and I discussed what time he would be picking me up on the Saturday. There was a new restaurant in town and we were going to try it out.

"Ooh," Sam said, "It looks wonderful there, I'm dying to try one of their curries."

Joe looked at her. "You'd better come with us then."

I really needn't go on. It's the age-old story, two's a couple and three's a crowd. By the end of the evening at the restaurant I felt that *I* was the gooseberry and when we came home from the zoo on the Sunday it was me who sat in the back of the car and Sam who sat in the front.

I didn't go out with Joe again and Sam ignored me at school.

So Sara wasn't the first person who I might have been mistaken about, and it seemed that I hadn't learned any lessons either from the Sam incident otherwise I might not have been taken in so readily by Glen.

"So what do I say?" I asked Russ now.

"It's simple," he said. "Tell her you haven't seen me. What's her surname, by the way?"

"McGrath," I said. "Soon to be Bracken."

Russ tutted and scowled at me. "She is not, and never was, going to be my wife."

"Okay, I believe you." And I did. He seemed so genuine, so sincere, that I couldn't believe he was lying. But then I also had trouble believing that Sara was lying.

"Well, do you know anyone called McGrath?" I asked.

"He shook his head. "No. But then if it was a put up scenario, they'd probably use false names. Where did they live?"

"Out of town," I said, "By the river."

I could see the cogs clicking in place in Russ's brain. "Big house?" he asked. "White pillars either side of the door? Big white gates?"

"That's right," I agreed. "So you *do* know her."

"Not her, no. But the guy that lives there is called Ben Reacher. He's co-director of Demain's computer business and Demain's right hand man."

"Oh." I realised that in this conversation I was still consistently using the single-syllable-sentence as acknowledgement that I'd heard what was said to me, and to give myself to assimilate what I was being told. The trouble was that at this particular moment I was being asked to assimilate a bit too much information.

So it was beginning to look as though Sara was a fraud and I had been completely taken in.

Again.

But hey! What if it was *Russ* who was the fraud? If I could be taken in by Sara then I was just as liable to be fooled by the man who had trespassed into my flat without permission.

"How did you get here?" I asked. "I mean how could you be sure of not being seen?"

I wore this." He pulled a false beard from his pocket. "And this." He pulled his scarf out from round his neck and I realised what a stupid question I'd asked. In Alaska, in winter, nobody could be recognised by the

83

way they looked – at least, not out of doors, they'd be too well wrapped up for any part of their body to be seen except their eyes. It was body shape and language that would give away someone's identity.

"I had to take a chance," Russ continued. "It's been quite a few weeks now and I really didn't think that they'd watch the apartment at all, but I couldn't be sure. I didn't think they'd watch it 24/7 though, but I couldn't hang around in the hallway for long, just in case, so I tried my key and was amazed to see that it still worked."

"Yeah, well you can thank the dear landlord for that," I said, "he was obviously too tight to pay for a new lock when he fixed the door. Either time."

"Either time? It was only broken down once. The first time I was stupid enough not to have the chain on when I opened the door to those two goons. The second time, when they did break down the door, was after I'd told the police I had copies of the photo."

"And the third time," I told him, "was when they broke in after I moved in."

"What?" he was shocked. "Were you hurt?"

I shook my head. "No. Luckily I wasn't here. But I was nearly hurt the next time they decided to attack, and that time it wasn't the flat that was assaulted."

This time Russ jumped up, a look of horror on his face. "I had no idea. Oh, my God, I'm so sorry. Honestly, I never intended for anyone else to get involved in my mess. What happened?"

I told him of the attacks on me, both of them, although I was now convinced that the attack that had happened outside the flat had been one of Glen's mates trying to get the ring off of my finger.

Russ was aghast, and I was glad to see it. Even if he was innocent in all this, it was still down to him that I'd been attacked and my flat broken into. I didn't see what he could have done to have avoided it, but that didn't stop me wanting to see him suffer just a little bit.

"I am so sorry," he said again.

"Oh," I suddenly remembered. "Your wife – sorry, ex-wife, has written to you a couple of times."

"I know," he said, "I've been in touch with her and she did say she'd written. How did you know that they were from her?"

"We opened them," I said, feeling a little sheepish. Wasn't it a crime to open somebody else's mail? "But we needed to find you," I said, justifying my behaviour. Then I was sheepish again. "Or I thought we did. I thought little Tommy needed a dad."

"He's probably got one already, even thought it might not be the same man that conceived him. He'll probably be brought up by a gangster and a gangster's moll and will turn out just like his dad," Russ said dryly.

"Oh, don't say that." I couldn't bear to imagine that cute little nose of Tommy's being spread across his face by a well aimed fist, and that was the sort of thing that would happen if what Russ said came about.

"Okay, I wont, but it's probably true. Anyway, I can see why you'd open the letters. Do you still have them?"

I shook my head. "Sorry, Sara's got them. Oh, and there were letters from your friend, James, as well."

"I see. Anyone else?"

"Nope, that was it; the others were all flyers, you know, mail-shots and stuff."

"As I said, I'd been in touch with my ex-wife, but not with James. Can you get the letter back for me sometime if at all possible, please? I'd like to read it, although at the moment I've got plenty to occupy me."

"So what are you going to do now?" I wanted to know.

"I don't know," He looked hopefully at me, "What do you suggest?"

"Hell, I don't know. It's nothing to do with me, don't involve me."

"But you are involved," he said quietly, "for which I'm very sorry,"

"But I don't want to be." I hopped down from the stool and went through to the kitchen where I switched on the kettle before returning to the main room of the flat. "Can't you tell them it's nothing to do with me?" I pleaded. "Tell them I know nothing and I'm not worth pursuing?"

"Tell who?"

"I don't know. The next time you're beaten up just tell them to leave me alone." Gosh, that sounded callous, but I was really feeling fed-up. Through no fault of my own I'd become involved with gangsters and their molls; people were attacking me, breaking into my home and now I'd got an intruder who was on the run from them as well.

At least *I* wasn't on the run, I thought. Then another thought struck me. Perhaps I should be? If anyone *was* watching the flat they'd now know I'd had a visit from Russ and would probably think that I was in cahoots with him. Damn, this was just going from bad to worse.

Suddenly I longed to be home; yearned for the green rolling fields, for cattle grazing in the meadow, for summer days and winter nights. Actually, I just wanted to be anywhere that wasn't here. I wish I'd never met

Glen, never crossed the ocean to live with him, never rented this flat – sorry, apartment. Everything came down to Glen somehow. Everything that had gone wrong for me in the past year was in his fault.

But no, that wasn't fair. It wasn't as though he'd kidnapped me and tied me up and stowed me in his luggage to bring me here. I had come of my own free will. And Glen, he was another example of my bad character judgement. I'd thought he was the real thing. Maybe I couldn't be blamed for that though, he had, after all, been putting on an act to entrap me, just as Sam had, in my schooldays, and Sara, from the recent past.

So was Russ putting on an act as well? Was everything he'd told me been a pack of lies?

I yawned and looked at my watch. It was gone midnight and I had to be up for work in the morning.

Russ noticed. "Sorry," he said, getting up, "It's late, I must be going." He stood up.

Was that it then? Was he just going to breeze into my life, turn my world upside down and breeze out again? I didn't think so.

"What are you going to do now?" I asked. "You must have some plans."

"I haven't decided," he said, pulling gloves out of his pocket. "It could be that I approach the police down in Anchorage. That's where the crime was committed, after all. I just don't know who to trust. All I ask of you is that you don't tell Sara I've been here or that you've heard from me. Play along with her if you like, but if you want my opinion I'd knock that friendship on the head. She's just using you, trying to get to me."

Was she? I still found it hard to believe.

"Look," I said, "I know I said this has nothing to do with me, but, as you quite rightly pointed out, I am already involved." I picked up my cell 'phone from where he'd left it on the sofa and scrolled through for my number – I could never remember it. Grabbing a pen and notepad from the shelf I wrote down my number, tore off the sheet and handed it to Russ. "Please keep me informed of what's happening," I said, "and I'll start reading the papers and making sure you haven't been found floating in a river or something."

He gasped.

"Sorry, I shouldn't have said that, I'm a bit overwrought." Well, I was, but it was still tactless of me to remind Russ of the danger he was in.

"It's true though, it could happen if Demain gets wound up enough." He smiled wryly. "Wont do him any good though; I've got copies all over

86

the place with friends and one with the bank, in an envelope to be opened if I die."

"No, but still better for you if he doesn't get that wound up," I said, as I opened the door to let him out."

"True. I will keep you informed though." He tucked the paper with my number on in his pocket, nodded goodbye, and he was gone.

And you're about as stupid as I am, I thought as I closed the door behind him. *I* know I'm on the side of right, but how did he know I wasn't one of the baddies? He shouldn't trust me any more than I trusted him. I made my mind up there and then to trust nobody in future.

CHAPTER FOURTEEN

Before I went to sleep that night I sent a text to Sara inviting her to dinner at the Apollo on Christmas Eve. It had turned out that when Mum and Dad booked the hotel they'd also booked a table in the restaurant for six on both the 23rd and 24th of December. My parents always had been sensible, I don't know why that particular gene hadn't found its way down to me, but nobody had ever called me sensible. Anyway, they'd realised that as close as that to Christmas they couldn't take a chance on getting extra seats at their table and, of course, they'd assumed that there'd be at least four of us because they'd expected Glen to be with us. And they'd thought we'd like to bring friends.

My parents were very caring, considerate people. No wonder I loved them. None of this "we're here to see you, we don't want to share you with *your* friends, we want you to ourselves" like the parents of some of my friends would react. And who could have blamed them if they'd said that? They hadn't seen me for months and they were here at what was traditionally a family time of year, yet they were still happy for me to have friends around me, people that my parents didn't even know.

So, an invite to Sara for Christmas Eve and notes pushed under Nat and Cindy's doors inviting them for either night. I didn't expect either of them to be free, I was sure the pole dancing club would be needing Cindy's expertise for both nights in this festive season, and I wasn't sure what gigs Nat's band was booked for, but if he hadn't got a gig then he'd probably got a hot date lined up anyway.

Once in bed I didn't sleep well. I tossed and turned and wondered about who was lying and who wasn't. Russ had seemed very sincere but then so had Sara. How could Sara be using me, she was a mum, and had little Tommy to prove it.

But did she? Could I be sure that little Tommy was even hers? Perhaps she'd borrowed him from somebody. No, surely nobody would lend anyone a baby just a few weeks old. But if what Russ said was true then these people were gangsters then I didn't know *how* gangsters would behave, never having been involved with any. I didn't think that Glen qualified to be called a gangster, despite his thieving ways; he was just a sad druggie with a major problem.

I didn't feel like going to work the next day. I was tired, confused and cold. But it had to be done. The office would be closed tomorrow,

Christmas Eve, so it was my last day for over a week because I'd tagged three days vacation on to the Christmas break.

I was careful though. I double-checked that the door was locked when I left and made a mental note to get the locks changed. Con obviously wasn't going to pay, he'd been too tight to buy new locks when the door had been damaged so he wasn't going to replace them just because Russ had simply used his own key to enter the room. I'd have to fork out for the replacement myself, but it was a small price to pay if it gave me peace of mind.

Unfortunately it wouldn't though, would it? Assuming that at least part of what Russ had told me was true, there were people looking for photographs and CDs with data on them and I didn't think that they were yet convinced that they weren't hidden somewhere in my flat. Replacing the locks wouldn't ensure that I didn't get another break in. They'd just break the door down.

I sighed as I pulled on my gloves and tightened them round my sleeves. Life was just too complicated sometimes.

When I switched my cell on at lunch time (we weren't supposed to have them switched on while we were working although I knew some people did, I'd see them with their heads down and playing with something in their laps, and I'd guess they were texting – at least, I *hoped* that was what they were doing), I had a reply from Sara. She said that she'd love to join us for dinner the following evening, Christmas Eve, and that her parents would baby-sit Tommy and her dad would drop her off at mine at six o'clock.

I also had a rather worrying voice mail from Russ, in which he said that he'd tried to get in touch with both his ex-wife and his friend, James, when he left me last night and that there had been no reply from either of them. "Because you said Sara had the letters, and therefore the addresses, I was concerned for them," his voice told me, "I should have rung them the minute you told me but I didn't. I don't for one minute expect that it would have made any difference though. As I said before, I had been in touch with her and warned her that there might be people looking for me and they might well approach her. I never thought to mention James though. I didn't think that anybody up here might know of his existence but now, of course, they do if they've got the letters from him. I'm heading down to where they live later."

Now I felt guilty. If we hadn't opened those letters then Sara wouldn't have known about his wife and James.

Hang on though, these were not only criminals, they were *clever* criminals. Surely they would have tracked down his wife and probably James as well without my interference? I sighed. I'd just made it easier for them, hadn't I?

I sent a text to Russ and asked him to continue to keep me informed. Then I replied to Sara's text and told her that I was looking forward to seeing her. Not entirely the truth, of course, but I didn't want her to suspect anything.

I hadn't decided how I was going to play the meeting with Sara. I was pretty sure that I wasn't going to mention having seen Russ. I wasn't convinced by any means that he was telling me the truth, but neither could I be sure that he was lying. I no longer had any faith in my own judgement and I really didn't think I could take any chances. Okay, so the people who kidnapped the child had returned her unharmed, but not before they got their hands on an awful lot of money. And rumours were rife about Carl Demain, he was said to have committed crimes much more serious than kidnapping, but was too wily a customer to leave any traces that would allow the cops the to arrest him. Oh, they'd hauled him in once or twice, but only for questioning, they'd never managed to actually prove he had been involved in anything since his original arrest when he was in his twenties. He was in his mid-forties now, older and wiser, more cunning and, somehow, more evil.

I finished my soup, switched off my cell and returned to work.

Nat knocked on my door just after I returned from work that evening. I'd already picked up a note from Cindy saying that she would have loved to have met Mum and Dad but that she was working. Perhaps she'd be able to meet up with them after Christmas? Good idea, I thought. Everything would be calmer after Christmas. Except, perhaps, my life.

"So," said Nat, walking into the room, "Give it up, hun. Who's the new fella in your life?"

"Huh?" If there was a new fella in my life I must have missed it.

"You bought a guy home late last night. I heard you talking when I got home. Couldn't hear what you were saying, although I put a glass up to the wall," he grinned, "Not really. But I did hear a male voice and decided you must have got yourself a new boyfriend – hopefully an improvement on the old one."

I shook my head. "That was no boyfriend, that was my predecessor."

"Your predecessor?" He looked puzzled, then suitable startled. "What, you mean the guy that lived here before? Russ?"

I nodded. "Yep. Russ Bracken."

Nat sunk to the sofa in disbelief. "What the hell did he want? "

I grinned at him, said "Make yourself comfortable, why don't you?" finished taking off my outdoor clothes and went through to the kitchenette to put the kettle on.

Back in the living area I sat down next to Nat, who was still looking bemused.

"Our friend Russ Bracken is involved in a crime," I said.

"What? I knew he was no good. Why didn't you tell me, hun? I could have come and beaten him up for you."

"Yeah, you probably could've, but it really wasn't necessary." I moved round in my seat and put my legs up across Nat's lap. "Ah, that's better. Anyway, it seems that Russ, while involved in a crime, is an innocent party."

"Oh, yeah?" Nat said disbelievingly.

"Oh, yeah," I said, imitating him. Then I corrected myself. "Well, I *think* so."

I proceeded to tell Nat what Russ had told me the previous evening. He threw in a few questions, but for the most part listened patiently.

When I'd finished, he gave a low whistle. "Phew. So that Sara you've been hanging around with isn't who she says she is at all? And those goons who jumped you in the alley were working for Carl Demain. And the guys who broke into the flat were working for him too? What about the guy outside, the one you thought might have been after your ring. Do you still think that he was something to do with your ex?"

I pondered for a moment. "Yeah, I do," I said, "the goons in the alley did a lot of talking; they were desperate to find Russ, and the guys who broke in here were obviously looking for something. That guy outside though, he didn't say a word, just grabbed my hand and ripped off my glove. He knew what he was after and the probability was that he knew the rings would be there because Glen had told him. I don't think he was involved in this." I looked at my fingers, relieved that I hadn't lost either of my two most treasured possessions; the one because it linked me back through several generations of my ancestors, and the other because I couldn't look at it without remembering my 18th birthday party which, in turn, reminded me not only of my family, but also all the friends that I'd grown up with and who now were so far away.

"Okay," Nat said, interrupting my thoughts, "and Russ went to the cops and believes it was the information he gave them that resulted in someone breaking in here."

"And look for photos. Yeah."

"So why doesn't he go to another police department somewhere else?"

"I think he will," I said. "As I said, he's down Juneau way at the moment and I think he may call in to the department down there."

"And he's down there because his ex-wife's gone missing?"

"And his friend, James. And, oh, Nat, I think it may be my fault?"

A frown creased Nat's brow, "Your fault? How's that, hun?"

I swivelled round and put my feet back on the floor. "Well, it was me who gave the mail to Sara to open, and me who let her keep the letters. So she had the addresses, do you see? Then she could give the addresses to whoever these bad people are and they could go and … and… Oh, Nat, I'll never forgive myself if anything's happened to them." I buried my face in his warm, woolly jumper and let everything wash out of me in the tears that suddenly flooded from my eyes. All the events of the last few months came flooding out in that sudden moment of despair.

Nat was a lover, not a comforter, but he did his best, patting me gently on the back and saying "There, there," at regular intervals. I could feel his discomfort through his clothes but it didn't stop me bawling or making his jumper sodden with my tears.

I groped blindly for the box of tissues that were on the arm of the chair, grabbed a bundle and wiped my eyes,

"Sorry," I mumbled, once I was able to speak again. "I don't know what happened."

"That's all right, hun." Nat was beginning to find his equilibrium now that the tears had stopped flowing. "You just let Uncle Nat take care of you."

"Huh. You couldn't take care of a bluebottle." I smiled through my tears as I pulled away from him, the misery gone almost as quickly as it arrived.

"But I'm good at making drinks," he said, jumping from the sofa. "Coffee? Or something stronger?"

I nodded. "Coffee, please."

While Nat made the coffee I gathered myself together, flung the used tissues in the bin and went through to the shower room to wash my face and hands.

"From what you said," Nat said, as I stood in the doorway to the kitchenette and watched him make the coffees, "You're convinced that Sara's not who she claims to be. You blamed yourself for letting her read and keep the letters."

"Oh, I don't know, Nat. I'm not sure what I believe now."

"Best play it by ear then, hun. Don't do anything rash, just go with the flow." He picked up the coffee mugs. "I can come to dinner tonight, by the way," he said as he followed me back to the sofa.

"I thought you had a 'hot date'?"

"She's ill," he said, "Rang this morning."

"Oh, so we're second choice are we?" I grinned, to let him know that I was joking.

"Not at all. I would probably have cancelled the date anyway, just so I could meet your folks?"

"Yeah, sure you would. Anyway, that's great, Nat. They'll love you. I'll make it clear to them that you're not prospective son-in-law material though. Oh, and you'd better change your jumper."

He looked down at his clothes. "I was going to get changed anyway," he said, "I'd hardly come to meet your parents dressed in scruffy jeans and jumper, would I?"

"Why not? Glen did. The first time he came to dinner at my parent's house his jumper had holes in the elbows and his jeans were worn at the knees. He looked like a brickie that had come straight off the building site. It was one of the reasons mum and dad didn't like him, because he didn't feel he had to make an effort."

"I can understand that. I must admit that if I meet them again then *I* probably wouldn't make an effort, but I do think that first impressions count."

Even in what he called his scruffy clothes Nat never looked less than immaculate. He always looked as though he thought that the love of his life might appear at any moment and he wanted to be ready for her if she did.

So Nat and my parents tonight for dinner, that would be great. Nat was easy to get on with and my parents were pretty cool, too. It was tomorrow night that would cause the problems. It would be interesting to see what my parents, who were probably a better judge of character than I was, made of Sara. It would be difficult for me though, to carry on as though everything was fine between us.

CHAPTER FIFTEEN

Dinner with Nat and my parents went perfectly, just as I had known that it would. They loved Nat and he loved them. "Your old lady reminds me of Meg Ryan," he said later. I didn't think that mum would take kindly to being called old, but I could see what he meant. Meg Ryan nearly always played vivacious, cheerful characters, and that described mum down to a T. I'd briefed them on the "phone and made sure that neither she nor my dad would think there could be anything going on between me and Nat, so there were no surreptitious questions about "prospects" or "intentions" the way that parents all over the world are inclined to slip in when they thought they might be speaking to their daughter's intended. So they relaxed and enjoyed Nat's company.

I must say I was impressed with Nat. I'd only ever seen him in the company of his peers before, his language, like theirs, often peppered with obscenities, his vocabulary colourful and colloquial.

Earlier that evening when I'd knocked for him I'd been bowled over by his appearance. I didn't know he *owned* a suit, yet alone would consider dinner with my parents an important enough occasion to actually *wear* it! His hair was neatly combed and not sticking up all over the place the way it usually was, and his boots polished to an incredible shine. He saw me admiring the way he looked and held out his hands for inspection. "Clean," he said with a grin.

I laughed. "You'll do," and punched him on the arm in friendly fashion. He closed his door and we made our way down the stairs and out into the frosty air.

I kept stealing sideways glances at Nat. He really was very handsome, I thought, and wondered if he'd ever settle down enough to make good husband material. Not for me, you understand, I had no designs on him; we were too good as mates apart from anything else. But I had seen various sides of Nat, I'd seen him with the band, all of them loud and leery, I'd seen him concerned when he thought I'd been hurt, and I'd seen him brave when I was being attacked. I'd known him as a friend and seen him as a friend to others and I knew that he was a man of many facets, not all of them obvious until you dug under the surface.

But Nat was also a womaniser. Not in a "love "em and leave "em" kind of way, he didn't go around breaking hearts. Well, maybe he did, but I didn't think it was his fault. From what I could gather – and I'd heard this from his girlfriends, not from Nat, so it was probably true – he always made it very clear from the start that he didn't 'do' commitment and that anything between them would be temporary, but fun. So the girls knew what they were letting themselves in for and it seemed to suit most of them as well as it did Nat.

There were exceptions, of course there were. Men and women alike sometimes heard what they wanted to hear rather than what was actually said, and often *didn't* hear what they would rather not know. There had been one girl, before I arrived, who had pestered Nat for months. Every time he or Cindy left the apartment block she'd be standing across the road, in all kinds of weather —mostly snow, it has to be said, and would run across and beg Nat to take her back or plead with Cindy to ask Nat to do the right thing. Eventually she'd stopped coming; suddenly one day she wasn't there. Nat, being Nat, had been concerned about her and had made enquiries through friends of friends and discovered that while she'd been doing her standing around in the road outside, she'd been chatted up by some guy, had started going out with him and they were now engaged!

"She was a nut," Nat had said when I asked him about her, Cindy having given me only the basic details, "I just hope the poor guy finds out before he commits to spending the rest of his life with her." Maybe she was slightly mad, but Nat just didn't realise what a catch most girls would consider him, he was too modest for his own good sometimes.

Anyway, that night he was on his best behaviour. Not a swear word passed his lips, he used the right cutlery for the right courses, he was politeness itself to my parents, courteous to Dad and flattering to mum, without being over-the-top.

Sometimes I caught mum looking from Nat to me and wondering why I couldn't have hitched my star to someone like him instead of that no good Glen. I knew she wouldn't really have wanted that though. I knew that somewhere deep inside her was a part of her heart that was pleased I was no longer with Glen because it meant that her little girl would be coming home soon.

There was lots of talk about the weather, mum loved the snow but she hated the long nights. I told her she should have come in the summer when we had over 21 hours of daylight instead of the current four. Dad told Nat about England, how cold it had been when they left and how they hadn't thought it could get much colder until they arrived in Alaska. We touched briefly on politics, on the forthcoming elections in America and how remote from the heart of things it felt in Alaska – almost like another country. Mum and Dad told Nat stories of Con when he was little, their distaste for the man he had become evident in the wistfulness of their memories. Nat talked of his parents, of how life had become difficult after his dad's stroke, but that they were comfortable now and managing. I knew that Nat sent them money from time to time, when he got a royalty cheque or when the band had a good paying gig, but he didn't, of course, mention that.

I wished Cindy could have been there. I was sure mum and dad would have liked her as well. She was so homely, so girl-next-door, that there was really nothing about her that they could *dis*like. I'd have to warn them though, about her job.

Somehow Nat made his song-writing and band-playing career sound respectable when he talked about it that night. I knew it was, of course, I was aware of what long hours Nat put in, and had some idea of how much he was earning – an amount which put my salary to shame. But I also knew that many people would view his occupations as those of a time-wasting lay-about. Luckily my parents weren't that old fashioned. They'd grown up in the seventies, fast on the heels of the swinging sixties, and they understood musicians and their way of life. I vaguely remembered Dad telling me that he'd been in a band when he was younger, and I guessed he was envious of Nat making a living by music,

The evening ended too soon. When I told mum and dad that Sara would be joining us the following evening I saw Nat shoot a glance at me but I wouldn't look his way, so his questions had to wait until we were walking home.

"I thought you'd decided to steer clear of Sara," he said. "What on earth possessed you to introduce her to your parents?"

"I hadn't said I'd made a decision," I protested, "Just that I wasn't sure." Neither had I told Nat previously that Sara was coming to dinner with me and my parents, so I could understand why he'd been surprised at that little revelation.

"I just don't know, Nat. I don't know who to trust or who is genuine. I'm just – as I think *you* suggested – going with the flow and seeing what happens.. I'm giving Sara a chance, if you like, to either trip herself up or to convince me she's genuine."

"Okay, do that, but be careful, won't you, hun?"

I promised him I would and he waited while I let myself into my apartment and didn't enter his own until I turned and said goodnight, having first checked that everything looked the same

I woke late the next day. The dark mornings were great for sleeping late; there was no light pouring through the window to wake me at some unearthly hour. Obviously what they weren't good for was getting up on workdays. I'd only been late to work once since I'd been here, and that was because one of the roads on my route to work had been closed and I'd had to find another way round. There were many times though that I arrived at work dishevelled, having jumped out of bed half an hour earlier, showered quickly and dressed before rushing off to work, usually before combing my hair and certainly before putting on make up. Apart from anything else, it took so long to dress, there were so many layers to wrap around me to keep me warm in those sub-zero temperatures. I loved Alaska, but I'd love it even more if the winters weren't so cold.

In those few minutes between waking and actually daring to get out of bed I had an idea. I grabbed my cell 'phone from beside my bed and sent Sara a text. If she really was who she said she was then she would surely have some photos of her and Russ together. I couldn't remember how long she'd said that they'd been going out together, but it was obviously over nine months if little Tommy was anything to go by, and most people have their picture taken if they're a couple, don't they? If only to prove to their mates what a good-looking partner they'd managed to snare. So I told Sara that I wouldn't know Russ if he turned up and was it possible for her to bring some photo's of them with her that evening. If what Russ had said was true and if Sara wasn't who she said she was then I expected Sara to text back and tell me she didn't have any photos. Because if she wasn't really Russ's girlfriend then she wouldn't, would she?

I'd got out of bed, padded to the kitchen, made myself a coffee and got back into bed, an extra jumper on for warmth before she replied. Her text read *Sure, I'll bring some with me. C U l8er. S x*

Damn! That blew that idea right out of the window. So did that mean that the Russ I'd met wasn't Russ at all but was, in fact, just one of the bad guys trying to get in my good books in the hope that he'd find out whether I knew anything about the real Russ and his damning photographs or not? This whole thing was getting weirder and weirder by the minute and I needed to talk it through with someone. Not my parents, obviously, they'd only worry and, besides, they didn't know any of the background. Not Nat either, he wouldn't surface until midday. Only one person left then. Cindy.

I knew that Cindy had been working until about three that morning but when she opened the door to me at nine that morning she looked as though she'd had a good eight hours sleep. And I knew she'd been out already that morning because I'd heard her come in while I was drinking my first coffee of the day.

We exchanged the normal pleasantries, Cindy made us a drink and I launched into recounting the events of the last few days, including Sara's and my texts of this morning.

"Wow!" Was the only comment Cindy could manage for a few minutes, then she bombarded me with questions similar to the ones Nat had asked the previous day as she tried to piece all the pieces together in her mind.

"So if she's got photos of her and Russ," I said eventually, "that means that the guy who turned up at my apartment *wasn't* Russ after all."

"What did he look like?" Cindy asked.

"Not very tall, about half an inch taller than me; red hair, greenish eyes, looked worried."

"Sounds like Russ," Cindy confirmed. "Well, not the worried bit, I don't remember that, but the fella who lived in your apartment before you certainly had red hair and he wasn't overly-tall either. Of course, they could have got a look-alike, or someone who was prepared to colour their hair, I can't really say. But you seem to think he was genuine?"

I shrugged. "I have absolutely no idea, Cindy. I've finally realised that I'm not too good at judging characters and I no longer take first impressions at first value. Sure, he *seemed* genuine enough, but a good actor – or even a mediocre one – could have carried that off easily enough if he knew his lines."

Cindy sighed. "I don't know what to advise you, sweetie. I'd be inclined to go to the police if I were you. After all, you got on okay with Chris Harrington after the break-in, why not give him a ring?"

It took me a moment or two to realise who she was talking about, and then I remembered that she'd been to school with the cop who spoke to me after the break in and yes, he had been nice. Sympathetic and kind then, just as he had been after I was attacked. But I really didn't want to involve the police, just in case the Russ I'd met was the real one and was telling the truth. I told Cindy this and she, like Nat, suggested I just "act normal and see what happens."

We talked of other things then, Cindy was always full of tales of the punters at the clubs in which she performed, and it was 11.30 before I realised what the time was.

"I'm meeting Mum and Dad at 12.00," I said. "We're going to hit the shops one last time and see what bargains we can grab."

Cindy glanced out of the window at the falling snow. "Rather you than me," she said. "Tony's coming to pick me up and we're going back to his. He's got a log fire and a furry rug."

"Too much information," I laughed as I left her flat. I rushed back into mine and put on coat, scarves and both pairs of gloves before venturing out into the Christmas Eve snow.

CHAPTER SIXTEEN

We had lunch in a diner in town, Mum and Dad wanting to get more of the ambience of the town rather than the cosmopolitan atmosphere of the hotel, then we picked up a few bargains and generally enjoyed being together. They came into mine for a cup of tea then mum and dad went back to the hotel, mum for a nap and dad to catch up on the news and get himself a drink in the bar. Sara and I were meeting them in the hotel lounge around 6.30; Sara's dad was going to drop her off at mine about six. If he *was* her dad, of course.

She turned up on the dot of six, admired my outfit (newly bought that very day, it was a bottle green trouser suit with zipped top under which I wore a cream jumper. Over it I wore a body warmer and some waxed trousers, both of which I could discard once I was at the hotel.

I asked Sara about the photos and she pulled an envelope out of her purse – see, purse, not handbag, I was getting to know the lingo – and handed it to me. Inside was half a dozen glossy photo's, five of them featuring Sara and a guy and one of them of the guy on his own.

I looked at the face that stared back at me from the shiny paper. His hair was reddish, but not the same vibrant red of Russ's – if, indeed, it had been Russ who had visited the previous day. And the eyes of the guy in the picture were brown, not green. My visitor yesterday had looked at me through green eyes flecked with gold, probably the correct term for them would be hazel, I wasn't sure, but either way, they weren't the eyes of Sara's Russ.

So which one was the real Russ, I wondered? There was no way that I could tell, but I knew someone who could.

"Could I keep one of these," I asked Sara, "to remind me of what he looks like? In case he turns up," I explained.

"No," Sara snatched the photos and the envelopes back, "I'd rather you didn't." She put the photos back in her bag and looked at me. "They're all I have," she said softly, "of Russ."

"And little Tommy," I reminded her, "you've got him and *he's* part of Russ."

"And little Tommy," she repeated. "Of course."

I took my coat off the back of the door and wondered how I was going to get hold of one of those pictures.

Sara nipped into the loo and I had an idea.

I didn't own a camera, Glen had nicked and sold the one I bought with me from the UK, but I did have a camera phone, the fact that I always carried it with me meant that it had been safe from Glen's thieving fingers. I took it out now, undid the zip of Sara's bag, wincing at the noise it made, removed the envelope containing the pictures and tipped them out. I snapped the top one and returned it to the envelope. One would be enough. I only needed one to show to Nat and Cindy.

I'd just managed to replace the envelope in the bag and slide back the zip on Sara's bag when she emerged from the shower room. My hand was still withdrawing from the direction of the bag and she looked at it, then looked into my eyes, then glanced down at her bag – sorry, purse, a frown forming itself round her eyes. She said nothing, the frown disappeared and she turned to me as if nothing had occurred. "Ready?"

I picked up my coat from where I'd slung it on the back of the sofa, donned scarf and gloves and we were on our way.

"You've heard nothing from Russ then?" she asked as we picked our way through the icy pavements.

"No, I would have told you if I had. Anyway, why would I? He won't make contact with me, he's no need to." What an odd question, she'd never asked me that before. It had always been me who asked her if Russ had been heard from – why would he contact me, he didn't even know me? Perhaps I was just being paranoid and she was making conversation, but it did seem odd she'd ask me that the day after he, or someone claiming to be him, paid me a visit.

"What about you," I asked, "have you heard anything?"

"Not a thing. Nor from his ex or that James."

"How odd," I said, but I knew it wasn't really odd. She wouldn't have heard anything, would she, because she'd never written to them, only told me she had. Instead she'd probably despatched a couple of goons to their respective addresses, probably the same goons who'd tried to do me over in the alley that night, and goodness knows what their instructions had been.

No, it wasn't Sara who would have done the dispatching, I mustn't make her a stronger player in this game than she deserved, otherwise I'd never be able to stand up to her if I needed to.

And why was I worrying about Russ's ex-wife and his friend James? If the same two goons had set about them that had attacked me then probably both Mrs Russ and James could probably have overpowered their attackers. Of course, I didn't know what Russ's ex-wife was like, she might have been very frail, and so could James, come to that, but I was trying to absolve myself from some of the guilt I was feeling at thinking that it might have been me who put Carl Demain on their trail.

"They might be away," I said now, for want of something to say. "Lots of people go away for Christmas, don't they?"

"Both of them?" Sara asked.

"Possibly. They probably knew one another, like we said, and maybe when Russ and his wife split up then this James stepped in to comfort her. And perhaps comforting turned to friendship, and friends became lovers."

"You've got an imagination, you have," Sara said, but not in a light-hearted, joking sort of fashion, more in an exasperated kind of way. We were quiet after that until we got to the hotel and I made the introductions.

Dinner with my parents was fine. Sara behaved impeccably, but I could sense a kind of reserve about her, as though she was holding something back. Given the knowledge that I now had that could simply have been my imagination, of course. She was polite to my parents and answered all their questions in a friendly manner, but she never showed any interest in them, in their lives.

I found it exhausting watching everything I said in case I let slip that I'd met Russ. I had to think before I spoke in case I gave information away that I could only have known if I'd had direct contact with Russ.

I was itching to get the photo on my 'phone to Nat and Cindy and eventually I managed to slip up to my parent's bedroom when Mum realised she hadn't got her watch with her. I volunteered to fetch it for her. Once in the privacy of their room I quickly sent a text to both my neighbours and asked them if they recognised the picture I was forwarding. I hung around a bit waiting for a reply, but none was forthcoming. There wouldn't be, I should have known that, Nat was gigging and Cindy working, but that hadn't stopped me hoping.

While we were sitting in the hotel lounge sipping our after dinner coffee and nibbling the mints that had come with it Mum asked if I'd like to go to Christmas Mass. "I haven't been for years," she said, "Remember how we used to go every Christmas when you were younger, Laura?"

I did. I, like Mum, hadn't been to midnight mass for years. In fact I hadn't stepped inside a church for years except for hatches, matches and despatches.

"That would be nice, Mum. Will you come as well, Dad? We can go to the church along the road from my flat."

""" Course I will, love. It'll be just like old times."

Laura's dad came to pick her up at eleven. Although she hugged me when she left and wished me a happy Christmas, I felt her heart wasn't in it. Of course, if she *was* who she said she was then Christmas would be a sad time for her with her baby's father missing. Somehow I didn't think that was the problem though. Something had changed between her and me, and I didn't think it was just my paranoia shining through.

When she left Mum and Dad gathered their outdoor clothes and we took a slow walk to church. As we trudged through the snow, Mum on one side of me and Dad on the other, I felt as though I was seven years old and going to my first midnight mass. I nearly took hold of their hands, instead of linking arms. I imagined that if I had they would have lifted me and swung me, just as they had all those years ago. It had been snowing then, as I recall, but only a few flakes had fluttered down, unlike tonight, when thick, feathery flakes trembled in the icy air around us.

From the diners and restaurants on the opposite side of the road came the faint strains of Christmas music and as we drew nearer to the Church we could hear clearly the Christmas carols which were being piped into the street on this icy cold Christmas Eve.

This might – probably *would* – be the only Christmas I'd ever spend in Alaska, and it was perfect. The icing on the cake was that I was sharing it with the two people I loved most in the entire world. For the next 24 hours at least I was going to put to one side all thoughts of Russ, photographs, Sara, Carl Demain and the rest of the mystery surrounding me and my apartment, and just enjoy the holiday.

The service was wonderfully uplifting. The priest who took the service was jovial, the choirs' voices angelic, the sermon short and to the point and the mass itself was moving. The church, which had seemed very warm when we entered, maintained a good degree of that warmth so that we were comfortable throughout the service. There were moments of seriousness, as was right and proper, as we were reminded of those less fortunate than us, whose lives had taken them down rockier paths and we prayed for them, while giving thanks that our own lives were on relatively smooth, straight roads.

As we came out of church, feeling full of God's goodness, I saw the band's van go past, and Nat waving from the passenger seat. The van stopped and Nat jumped out, complete with guitar. He greeted my parents like long lost friends and we all exchanged Christmas greetings, for it was, of course, already Christmas day. Mum and Dad said their goodbyes and made their way back to the Apollo and I linked my arm through Nat's and we returned to the grey block in which we lived.

"Be it ever so "umble, there's no place like home," I quipped as Nat turned the lock on the front door.

"So true, hun, so true." Nat stood to one side to let me in and closed the door behind us, checking that the lock was dropped so no intruders could venture in.

I took the stairs two at a time. "It's Christmas, Nat. Isn't it exciting?"

"Hush," he scolded. "You'll wake everybody up."

"Oh, don't be such an old fuddy-duddy, Nat. It's Christmas, they're probably" – I hesitated before continuing in a much quieter voice, "-all awake anyway." It had finally dawned on me that not everybody got excited as I did about Christmas. Not everyone found it difficult to sleep because of the butterflies of excitement that fluttered in their bellies. For some people it was just another day, and even those who recognised its importance, not just for the religious factors but also for the whole family thing, even many of them would be safely ensconced in slumber at one o'clock in the morning.

"Sorry," I whispered as I turned and waited for Nat on the bend of the stairs.

"It's okay, hun," Nat came abreast of me. "Did you get my text?"

"Hell, no. My "phone's off." I'd switched it off as we entered the church and had forgotten to turn it back on. I grappled with my bag but Nat put out a restraining hand. "It's okay, it was just to say that no way is that a picture of the guy who used to live in your flat."

"No? Are you sure?"

"Positive."

We continued up the stairs, this new piece of information rocketing round in my brain.

At the top of the stairs I stopped, aghast. The door to my flat was open, and from the light from the landing, which snaked in through the door I could see that the place was a mess.

"Oh, shit! Not again." With no thought for my safety this time I barged into the room and switched on the light.

CHAPTER SEVENTEEN

The place was nearly in as bad a state as it had been on the previous occasion that it had been broken into; the only difference being that this time the curtains, carpet and mattress had been left intact. Elsewhere drawers had been emptied out, the entire contents of my wardrobe strewn across the bed, the stools at the breakfast bar tipped over, packets of food emptied, along with the contents of jars and altogether the whole scene just looked too daunting to contemplate.

I sunk to the sofa, my arms clutched tightly around my middle and rocked backwards and forwards as I tried to get my head round this latest violation of my own personal space. This was a place in which I should feel safe; it was my home, for God's sake. This didn't happen to other people, what had I done to make it happen to me?

In the background I was dimly aware of Nat opening his cell phone,

"Cindy," he said, "we've got trouble ..." then his voice faded out of my consciousness and for a while I went somewhere else, somewhere where I couldn't be reached, somewhere safe, warm and comforting. I stayed there, wrapped in a cocoon of unawareness until I felt Nat's arms lifting me to my feet. "Come on, hun, back to mine."

I allowed myself to be led unprotestingly to Nat's flat, where he took my outdoor clothes off of me before drawing back the comforter on his bed. He sat me down and removed my boots, then lay me back, fully clothed on his bed before covering me over. While I was dimly aware of what was happening I could no more stop it than fly. For the moment, at least, I was willing to let somebody else take control of my life, as long as that somebody was someone I trusted.

I was awake, gazing unseeingly at the ceiling, when Nat appeared by my side some minutes later.

"Coffee here if you want it, hun," he said, placing a mug of steaming liquid on the chair beside the bed which doubled up as a bedside cabinet. "Cops are on their way, but I'll deal with them, don't you worry." I tried to smile but couldn't. Nat patted me on my arm, he looked uncomfortable. I doubt he was used to having barely conscious women in his bed, usually the women who occupied the place where I now was were far livelier. But that was a thought I had later; at the time I had no conscious thought.

Surprisingly I slipped into sleep, but was awoken some time later by the sound of voices. The clock told me it was two o'clock, the room told me it was Nat's but for a blessed moment I couldn't remember why I was there. Surely Nat and I hadn't .....

Shit! No, we hadn't. In a way it would have been better if we had, even though it might have destroyed a beautiful friendship, it would still have been better than the reality.

Anger flooded into me as I recalled the break-in, giving me the impetus I needed to snap out of the numbness and think about getting moving and sorting things out in the flat.

Nat's apartment was no bigger than mine, so I could see at a glance that he wasn't in the flat and guessed that the voices I could hear beyond the door were the police.

I didn't trust the local police now, how could I after what Russ had told me? But there was no harm in acting like a normal citizen and reporting the break in.

At that moment the door opened and Nat entered. When he saw me awake he rushed over. "Hun, are you okay? I didn't think you'd be awake."

"I'm okay, Nat," this time I did manage a smile, even if it was one that trembled on my lips and threatened to fall into the abyss of despair that even now was hanging around ready to engulf me.

"The cops are in there," Nat said with an incline of his head in the direction of my flat.

I nodded. "I guessed."

"I tried to persuade them not to, but they want to speak to you, see if anything's missing, that kind of thing."

"Sure," I pulled myself up in the bed and, with Nat close behind me, left the flat and crossed the landing into my own apartment, where the mayhem seemed just as bad as last time I'd been here.

Two different cops this time, neither of whom I recognised. They took a statement from me, I told them that as far as I could tell there was nothing missing, and then they left, but not before warning me that they didn't hold out much hope of catching the perpetrators and that I should get my locks changed. Tell me something I don't know, I thought.

"Right," said Nat, as we stood at the window and watched the police getting into their car. "Here's what's happening. Tonight you're staying with me, in my bed, and I'll have the sofa." Tomorrow you're going to spend the day with your parents while I clear up in here," we looked around us at the absolute, total mess that had been my home and I wondered – as no doubt he did, too – where he was going to start. "Then," he continued, "when you return from a wonderful day in the bosom of your family, you're moving in with Cindy."

"But –" I started to protest and Nat laid a finger across my mouth. "No buts," he said. "Tony's picking Cindy up from work and they're off to his lodge for a dirty weekend." He grinned. "Good luck to them, that's what I say. Anyway, her flat's going to be empty for the next three nights, but if you'd rather stay in here with me rather than be on your own then that's fine, too. I just thought you'd prefer some privacy."

We all had keys to the others' flats. I had one to both Cindy and Nat's and they each had one to mine and to each other's. The flat only came with one key but we'd all had spares cut. Each of us was capable of losing a key or leaving it somewhere so it was a good safety fallback. Anyway, it made such plans as Nat was suggesting possible.

"If Cindy's flat's empty I could stay there for the rest of tonight," I suggested.

"No way, hun." Nat put an arm round my shoulders and gently steered me out of my flat, across the landing, and into his. "Tonight you're not going to be on your own. Ah, coffee's cold. Sit on the bed and I'll make us a fresh one."

I did as I was told and Nat took away the cold cup of coffee and clattered about in his kitchenette making a fresh one while I grabbed my bag and removed my cell from it. Switching it on, I retrieved Nat's text and also a couple from Cindy. The first one was to tell me that no, she didn't recognise the man in the picture I'd sent, the second one offering sympathy and the use of her apartment for as long as I wanted. Bless her.

Tucked up in Nat's bed, hearing him gently snoring on the couch, sleep evaded me. I tossed and turned, wondering what would have happened if I'd been in the flat when the break-in happened. I'd been lucky that time in the alley, I'd been able to take those goons by surprise, but this time they would have been ready for me and I'd be unlikely to be able to get away so easily from them again. They would probably have tortured me in an effort to get the information they wanted, pulled my fingernails out or something. Beneath Nat's thick comforter I shivered. It didn't bear thinking about.

Then I was struck by a thought. I didn't know what time the break-in had occurred, but I wouldn't mind betting it had been in the hour before I returned. The hour after Sara had left the hotel, knowing that I'd not be home until the service finished. Sara, who I now believed suspected something. I didn't know if she had realised that I'd been doing something with the photos and maybe she had guessed that I was suspicious of her.

On the other hand it wasn't impossible that someone had seen Russ come and go the previous day in which case they might consider they had good reason to ransack my apartment again in case Russ had passed something incriminating my way.

In which case they were probably following him now.

I sprung up in bed and grabbed my "phone again. Nat stirred, rolled over and continued snoring. Beneath the covers I sent Russ a text warning him that he may be being followed. If by any chance his ex wife and James *had* got away somewhere I didn't want Russ leading the goons to them.

His reply came back almost immediately: *Thought I had someone on my tail, think I've lost them now. Have heard from Pam (my ex) and she and J r safe. Have been to police in Juneau and reported. Keep in touch. R*

That was all right then. One less thing to worry about. Instead, I worried about leaving Nat to do the clearing up in the flat. I was so relieved that my parents had persuaded me not to do the present opening ceremony in my apartment, but to hold it in their room in the hotel. Their hotel room was near enough as big as my flat anyway and it was warmer and more comfortable. Although I'd really wanted to spend the time in my own flat, I had seen the sense and had already given them their presents to put under the small tree provided by the hotel management. If I hadn't I was sure that the gifts would have been unwrapped and broken and flung around my flat, instead of safely nestling beneath the tree, waiting to be unwrapped by eager hands later that day. The fact that it now meant that my parents wouldn't see the state of my flat and start worrying was an added bonus.

But it didn't seem fair to leave it all to Nat to sort out. Apart from anything else I was oddly reluctant to have him handle my underwear, even if it was only to put it all in a machine in the basement. Still, I wasn't due at the hotel until eleven, so I could get a certain amount done before I left and maybe only leave a small amount for Nat to do.

Luckily I knew Nat had no plans for the day apart from slobbing around. Normally he spent the season with his parents but they'd opted for a winter cruise and Nat said he'd been looking forward to a day on his own. I wasn't sure whether or not this was true, but he'd certainly turned down my invitation to join mum, dad and me at the hotel. His parents had sent him a new game for his Wii and I guessed he was itching to spend a whole uninterrupted day playing with it. Sadly I'd messed up those plans, at least for the early part of the day.

Eleven o'clock found me leaving the apartment block with my underwear washed, dried and back in the drawers and my clothes shaken. It wasn't practical to wash every item of clothing that I owned again even though I would have like to. Most of them had something between them and my skin when I wore them though, so it didn't feel as though there were any goons' vibes touching my skin directly. Stupid, perhaps, but like the sheets on the bed I wanted what touched my skin to be untainted.

"Forget what's happened here," Nat said as he saw me off, "if you can. Enjoy the day and the time with your parents. You'll be safe there, with them, and safe back here in Cindy's flat when you come home."

I had earlier admitted to Nat that I didn't think I'd ever feel safe in my own flat again. He said he understood and that he thought Cindy would be suggest that I stayed with her instead of moving back into my apartment. I didn't think that should be an option either really, not long term, and hoped that I'd feel safer in my flat once the locks were changed. That wouldn't be until after Christmas now; although locksmiths did operate over Christmas I guessed they'd charge the earth and, as long as I'd got somewhere to stay, it was an unnecessary expense. I might feel marginally safer, but they could still break in, locks hadn't stopped them this time, had they? Or last.

Nat and I had discussed how they'd gained entry into the department block and decided that they'd probably just walked in behind another resident. Although everyone in the block was friendly we tended to keep to ourselves, I didn't know, for instance, the names of anyone else with rooms in the building apart from Nat and Cindy. I knew lots of other people by sight though, and would nod and smile when I passed them on the stairs. One or two I'd strike up a conversation with if I met them in the basement, but I wasn't on first name terms with any of them, so it was quite feasible that if somebody looked as though they had a right to be there then a resident coming in or going out would even hold the street door open for them.

I didn't think I'd be able to forget what had happened quickly though, and I didn't, but I drank rather more than I normally would in my parent's company and pretty soon a haze fell around me which numbed the harsh edges of reality and lulled me into a false sense of security.

The events of the early morning hours aside, it was a wonderful, wonderful day. Mum and Dad seemed thrilled with the items I gave them, a blouse for mum which I'd sewn by hand on cold winter evenings spent alone in my flat and a book on fuschias for Dad. He was a fuschia nut and although I hadn't seen any growing in Alaska, I'd found several books that I didn't recognise and didn't think he'd have. A couple of CDs each, some smellies for mum and a scarf for Dad and that was them done.

They gave me a new pair of gloves, which I badly needed, a jumper I'd admired while we'd been in town a couple of days previously, and a cheque for £500. I was gobsmacked. They said they'd give me money and it would be for a decent amount, although not enough to buy my ticket out of here, and I was expecting around £200. This much, added to my savings, would probably get me home, I'd seen flights for around $900. I flung my arms round Mum when I saw how much the cheque was for and thanked her so very much, then did the same with Dad.

"We want you home," Mum said, reaching over from where she sat on the edge of the bed to pat my knee. "Selfish, perhaps, but we just want our little girl back with us." Was that a tear glistening in her eye? She rubbed a hand across her eye and I thought that yes, it probably had been.

"And I want to come home, too." I said, and realised how much it was true. It would be sad to leave Nat and Cindy, but they were only neighbours, ships that passed in the night, and I could keep in touch with them via email and texting. I would no longer be sorry to leave Sara of course, but I'd miss my job and the friends I had there, but on the other hand I hoped I'd soon be able to pick up with my old friends back home. What I *wouldn't* miss was the sense of danger that constantly surrounded me now.

I looked at the cheque again. "I won't be able to come just yet," I said.

"Of course not, love." Dad said. "The ticket prices over Christmas and New Year are astronomical. And you'll need to work your notice at your job. But we were hoping you'd maybe be back for Easter, perhaps?"

Easter ... spring ... lambs ... sun ... longer days ... and Mum's birthday. She'd be fifty in April, and I guessed she'd want me there for the celebrations. Even when I'd come out here, excitedly looking forward to a new life with my new love, I'd planned to make it home for Mum's 50th. Since splitting with Glen I'd begun to think I wouldn't make it in time, the money I'd hoped to subsidise my flight with had long since disappeared down Glen's throat or up his nose, but now the fantasy was becoming a reality.

"Oh, yes," I said, "surely by Easter."

I tucked the cheque – my passport into my future – into my purse, which went safely in my bag, "I can't tell you how grateful I am –" I began, but Mum stopped me. "It's a selfish present really, sweetheart. We just want you home. We would never have said this if you'd still been with Glen or, indeed, if you seemed as though you wanted to make Alaska your home. But you said you planned on returning, so we just thought we'd hurry things along a little bit. For us, as well as for you." They were definitely tears I could see now, and Mum grabbed a tissue and wiped her eyes.

"What your mum said," Dad said gruffly, and I knew that he, too, was battling with emotion. I hoped that if I ever had a child they didn't put me through what I'd so obviously put them through. Having a child halfway round the world with someone you didn't like must be a nightmare.

I had presents to unwrap from Nat and Cindy too, and Maisie from work. Chocolates, smellies and wine respectively. All very welcome and would be much enjoyed. I had more money from aunts and uncles in the UK and, together with the little I'd put aside in my "going home fund" I had around $1100 dollars, so knew I'd be going home soon.

It was with happy thoughts that I went down to dinner.

Dinner was scrumptious. The hotel had pulled out all the stops, and course followed course until at last, stuffed to the gills, we returned to my parents room with our coffees. The hotel lounge, although cheerful, was too crowded and too noisy and we just wanted to sit and relax, to play cards and to talk about the future.

CHAPTER EIGHTEEN

I slept surprisingly well that night, fortified by food and drink, and my dreams were peaceful and full of English greens and blues instead of Alaska's greys and whites.

When I'd got home I hadn't invited Dad in for coffee as I normally would. I don't think he noticed though, we were all tired, and I think he was looking forward to his bed.

I knocked on Nat's door, then had a quick peek into my flat. I was still standing there when I heard Nat's door open and his footsteps come up behind me. "Wow! Good grief, Nat, you've done an absolutely amazing job."

And he had. Before I'd left for the hotel that morning we'd had a quick breakfast of muffins and coffee then set to work. I'd got all my underwear washed and dried by 10.30 and Nat had hung everything back in my wardrobe and replaced drawers into their respective places and picked up everything that had been knocked over. Since I left he'd given the whole place a make-over, or so it seemed. The only indication that the place had been trashed the previous nights was the crack in the door surround, where the lock had given way. But that would be Con's problem, not mine.

"Con!" I said, "I have to let him know,"

"It's done, babe, I rang him this morning."

"Oh, Nat, you're too good to be true. What did he say?"

"Oh, you know Con, muttered about having let the criminal element into the block and groaned about the cost of things, but he'll do it, of course. He'll be round in the morning – or one of his sidekicks will, and they'll fix the door."

"Thank you, Nat. For everything. You've done wonders here, thank you ever so much."

"You're welcome, hun. Now, come and tell me about your day."

So I did. I gave him a blow-by-blow report of the other diners in the hotel, the presents I gave and received, the details of each course we had for dinner and the things we talked about.

It hadn't escaped my notice that the day Nat had been looking forward to spending playing with his new game had been ruined. "What can I do," I asked, "to make it up to you?"

I knew what the answer would be. Nat was not the world's greatest cook, in fact I think this morning's muffins and coffee was about as complicated a meal as he was able to prepare and he was constantly begging for invites to eat with me or Cindy. He didn't get that many as neither of us did that much cooking in our poky little kitchenettes, preferring to eat out a lot of the time, although as money was tight I was more often found scrounging meals off of friends and colleagues myself. Well, not scrounging, but if they were offered I wasn't going to turn them down, was I?

Sure enough, Nat put on his little boy lost look and said, "Can you feed me, missus?"

I punched him playfully, "You are so predictable, Nat. Yes, of course I will. I'll cook for you every night if you want."

Nat laughed and shook his head. "Just a meal now and then would be great."

"So what nights are you free?"

I didn't feel that cooking him a meal was really repaying him though as I would probably have fed him at least one night a week for my remaining time in Alaska anyway; I'd have to think up something else for him.

We arranged an evening and then relaxed on his sofa, a glass of wine for each of us on the occasional table.

"Nat," I said, picking up my wine and taking a sip, "I'm going home."

He looked puzzled. "You can't. The door's broken. I thought you were staying here or at Cindy's."

"No, you don't understand, Nat, I'm going home. To England."

"Hell, yeah, I know you are. But that won't be for ages yet, you're the pits at saving money."

I leant forward in my seat to where he was laying out on the bed. "I'm going home soon, Nat. My parents gave me the air fare."

Bless him, he looked really crest-fallen. "But you can't," he protested. "You said you would be here for ages."

I sat back into the sofa and put down the glass. "I know I did, but you can't really blame me, can you Nat? Living here hasn't been exactly a barrel of laughs for me, with the exception of getting to know you and Cindy of course."

Nat quickly recovered his equilibrium. "Aw, you spoil all my fun," he said, "Who's going to feed me now on the nights that Cindy works?"

I laughed. "You'll manage. Just like you managed before I moved in. Oh, and don't count on Cindy for too much longer, I've a feeling that she and Tony might tie the knot soon, or at the very least she'll move in with him."

Nat looked thoughtful. "You could be right. She's spending more and more time at Tony's lately and less time in the flat. Hell, I'm going to have to get my act together and get a few more lovely ladies at my beck and call."

"I should think you've got them lining up already," I said dryly and he grinned and winked at me and touched the side of his nose.

"That'd be telling," he said.

At midnight I took my empty glass and put it on the counter by the sink, rubbed my eyes and told Nat I was heading for bed in Cindy's.

"Okay, hun. They're clean sheets, she said, she changed them before she left. I'll walk across with you."

"What, across the landing? Nah, think I'll be safe enough doing that." I kissed him on the cheek, but I was glad that he stood watching in his open doorway until I switched on the light in Cindy's flat and closed her door behind me.

I woke at eight the next morning. As usual I checked my "phone when I woke and found a message from Russ: *Police in Juneau seem to believe that my photo is genuine and are digging deeper into the whole business. I have warned them about the local police and hopefully they'll keep them out of it. R U on my side yet?*

The last comment was fair enough. I'd made it clear to him that I found it hard to believe him when he'd told me that Sara was a fraud, and that I didn't necessarily trust him.

I replied to his text: Gd. *Hope they sort things out. On your side now. Apt. broken into again after I told Sara it wld be mty. Luck. L*

By telling him that the apartment had been broken into after I'd told Sara that it would be empty I believed he would realise that I no longer trusted Sara,

And I did wish him luck. I wanted this whole thing tidied up and put away before I left Alaska. I didn't want to sit at home wondering what was happening and whether they police had caught Carl Demain or whether he was still looking for Russ and, by proxy, for me. I wouldn't put it past him to track me down and take the trip to England to get at me.

In the meantime, I was going to make the most of having Mum and Dad here. They'd be gone in a few days time, and everything would feel a bit flat once they'd left. Oh, except for New Year's eve. Nat and I were going to my friend Maisie's party. Maisie was good fun and the evening should be a laugh. With any luck I would have booked my flight home by then and would use the evening to let everyone who needed to know, know.

I had to give a month's notice at work, but didn't see why I shouldn't be back in the UK by mid-February. My stomach lurched as I thought about it. It was fabulous, but just a little bit scary. Would I be able to pick up my old life where I'd left it a year ago? Would my friends have their own lives that no longer included me? Would I be able to get a job? Would I be able to live in the family home again after living independently? This last problem could be the hardest, I thought. Part of me longed to go to work and come home in the evening, hang my coat up and sit down to one of Mum's dinners. But I knew it wouldn't be that easy. I loved my parents to bits, and I know that they knew I did, but I thought I'd probably be looking for a flat or something that provided independent living quite soon after returning to England. Once you've been master in your own home – or mistress, come to that, it was hard living under someone else's roof, however well you got on.

We spent the next few days doing a lot of card playing in their room or watching television – Mum and Dad on the bed and me sprawled in the armchair. We had dinner in the hotel or in diners, and we also went to the theatre and an art museum and an Alaskan history museum. We visited churches and hot springs and dog lots and every evening we collapsed into our respective beds, but not before the Northern Lights put on a spectacular light show for Mum and Dad two nights on the trot.

On the 27th Cindy called. "Hi, sweetie. Just wanted to make sure you're safe and comfortable." We talked about the possibility of her coming home the next day and having dinner in the hotel with Mum, Dad and me and she thought it a good idea. "I'll stay over in the apartment that night, but from then on it's all yours," she said.

It turned out that I was right, she was moving in with Tony and giving up the flat. The rent was paid up until the end of January and she wouldn't hear of my repaying any of it to her. "After that it's up to you," she said, "but as far as I'm concerned you can stay as long as you want."

Mum and Dad liked Cindy just as much as they'd liked Nat, as I'd known they would. I dreaded them asking her what she did for a living, but when they did and Cindy told them she was a pole dancer Mum was fascinated. I sat, open-mouthed while Mum asked Cindy exactly what she did and what sort of money she earned and what were the punters like. She went on about the shoes, too. "They're coming back into fashion" she said, "all those high heels. They're wonderful, make a woman *feel* like a woman, if you know what I mean," Then she turned to me. "I'm thinking of taking pole dancing lessons, you know."

The jaws of all three of us listening dropped at that piece of startling news.

"What? First I've heard of it," Dad said, dropping his knife and fork to his plate with a clatter.

"Not in a club, silly," Mum said, giggling. "Pole dancing is all the rage now, didn't you know? Good for the figure. There are classes at the local adult community centre on a Wednesday morning. Thought I'd give it a try,"

"Oh, that's all right then," Dad resumed eating his meal and we followed his lead while I tried not to think of Mum in the same sort of pole dancing clothes that I'd seen Cindy in. Dad was probably trying not to imagine it too, but for different reasons.

"Laura tells us you're moving in with your boyfriend," Mum said to Cindy.

"Yes," Cindy proudly held out her hand so Mum could admire her sparkling new engagement ring. "We're getting married in October."

I'd made all the appropriate "ooh" and "aah" noises over the ring when Cindy had turned up at her apartment earlier that afternoon. I'd also commiserated with her at the fact that she was giving up her job.

"It will be too far to travel," she said. Tony lived 50 miles away. "And there are no clubs in his town. Well, there is one, but it's seedy and run down and I wouldn't want to work there."

"So what will you do?" I asked.

"Shorthand typists are always in demand," she said, "and computer operators, and I can do both."

"Really?" It was amazing what hidden talents some people had.

"Really," she agreed. "Tony doesn't really want me to work anyway, but I'd rather do that than sit at home twiddling my thumbs. At least until the bambinos come along."

I raised my eyebrows.

"Tony wants four," she said, "but I've told him that two will probably be enough. We'll see. I'm not against a big family, but they do make a lot of work."

I was happy for her; she and Tony seemed well suited. On the one occasion I'd met him he'd struck me as being a lovely man and he obviously adored Cindy. Tomorrow he would be collecting Cindy in the morning and taking her and her clothes and personal bits and pieces to his home. Which was good; I hadn't liked leaving all my bits in an unlocked flat and had moved most of my personal items into Cindy's apartment, so it was a bit overcrowded. I'd left most of my clothes in my own flat, it just hadn't been practical to move all of them, but I'd brought my underclothes and my bits of jewellery and a drawer-load of documents and paperwork.

I'd called Con and let him know that I was leaving my flat and that he could rent it out as soon as he wanted. I felt a bit guilty doing that, supposing some little old lady moved in and then the flat was broken into? Well, I'd be here for a while, so I'd keep an eye open. Once I'd gone it would be down to Nat to do his protective thing. Con moaned and groaned and complained I was leaving him in the lurch, but I pointed out that I'd paid up to the end of January and if he got his act together and repaired the door then he could rent out the apartment as early as next week, so he'd get double the rent on it for a whole month. He cheered up a bit after that.

Neither of us got much sleep on Cindy's last night. I was painfully aware that this was possibly the last time I'd see Cindy. We'd been like a family, her, me and Nat and I'd miss her. Nat would miss her more probably, he and Cindy went back a lot further, and with me going soon as well I felt quite sorry for him. He'd have to get to know a whole new batch of people in a relatively short time.

When we got back from dinner at the hotel that night we knocked on Nat's door and invited him to join us for a drink. When he saw the cramped conditions Cindy and I were spending the night in he suggested we enjoy our drinks in his apartment, so we all trooped back across the landing and Cindy and I settled on the sofa while Nat took the bed. We talked of everything and nothing, Nat and Cindy often referring back to times before I knew them. Shared memories.

At one o'clock Cindy and I staggered back into her apartment and climbed into our respective beds, but we didn't go to sleep. Cindy recounted incidents she'd experienced in the flat, like the time a dog got in from the street and spread his business around the place, or the row all the residents had with Con when he tried to put their rents up 20% in one go, and the time they had the police arrest someone on the first floor for murder. She reminisced about previous tenants, all gone now, most of them to the big tenement block in the sky, but some to other houses and homes, and one or two that had ended up in jail. There'd been some interesting characters according to her, like the ex-circus clown who gave impromptu shows on the landings, or the ex farmer who talked about nothing but his pigs, and the woman who wore purple and pulled a lead behind her that had nothing at the end of it. That hadn't stopped her talking to her dog, Blue, though.

117

Eventually our voices faded and the next thing I knew it was eight o'clock and Cindy was dressed and packed and ready to go.

"No point in waking Nat up," she said. "Give him my love and tell him I'll be in touch." They'd already discussed Nat going down to stay with Cindy and Tony at Easter, and I knew that they would continue their friendship for a long time to come, maybe for ever, and I was pleased for them, and a tiny bit jealous that I would no longer be part of that friendship once I returned to the UK. Oh, we'd write for a while, Cindy had given me her address, and of course I knew Nat's, and we'd continue to send Christmas cards long after the letters and emails had ceased, but a friendship, a *proper* friendship, wouldn't survive the miles and the ocean between us.

I got up and put on my thick robe and Cindy and I hugged for a moment.

"Gonna miss you," I mumbled.

"Gonna miss you, too, sweetie. But you'll be going home soon, so you've got loads to look forward to. I know you won't come, but I'll send you an invite to the wedding."

"You'd better," I told her. "I'll pin it to the wall and think of you every time I look at it. And especially on the day."

There was a knock on the door and Cindy opened it and flung herself into Tony's arms, where she stayed for a moment, enjoying their first kiss of the day. Eventually she pulled away and picked up the smallest of her three cases. Tony waved at me, picked up the other two and retraced his steps down the steps.

Cindy kissed me on the cheek. "Stay well and good luck. Keep in touch"

Then she was gone and I was in the flat alone.

CHAPTER NINETEEN

Two days later and Mum and Dad were gone, too. I felt like an orphan. I drove them to the airport and we stood in a group hug for ages, I was reluctant to let them go, but knew I had to. It was hard to hide my tears, but I didn't want their memory to be of me crying, so I took a deep breath and fixed a smile on my face.

Mum had no such compunctions, and the last view I had of her this side of the Atlantic was with rivulets of tears running down her face that she made no attempt to disguise.

I sat in the airport for hours, watching the spot in the sky where I'd last seen their plane, feeling empty and hollow inside. Eventually though I realised that the hollow feeling was caused more by my having missed breakfast than my parents departure and so I tucked into a hearty meal in the airport cafeteria before heading back to town and handing back the hire car.

I spent the rest of that day pottering round in the flat, writing letters home to let friends know that they'd soon be seeing me again and generally relaxing after the excitement of the last few days.

I got up late the next day and spent the afternoon with Nat; it was one of the days on which I'd promised to feed him, so I made a chicken pasta bake and with a sparkling white wine we felt quite bloated when we'd finished. Nat went back to his place then, to prepare for the party, and I did the same. An hour and a half later he knocked on my door and gave an appreciative whistle when I opened it. This would be my last chance to dress up in this country probably, so I'd gone the whole hog. My hair was freshly washed and the curls tamed by pinning most of my hair on top of my head, leaving just a few stray curls artfully framing my – although I say it myself – expertly made up face (I'd had a Saturday job at a beautician's while I was at school and though I seldom used the tricks of the trade I'd learnt nowadays, I remembered them). I had on my "little black number" that I hadn't worn since I'd lived in the apartment, sheer black tights and high heel shoes. I was gratified that Nat, who went out with some stunning women, could find me worth whistling at.

"You look *gorgeous*," he said.

"Thanks, Nat, and you don't look so bad yourself."

He didn't, but then as I've already said, Nat was a good looking guy who always managed to look respectable and, when he took the trouble to dress up a bit the way he had when we had dinner with my parents, then he looked like a male model, although somewhat more masculine than some male models that I'd seen.

A cab whisked us across town to where Maisie lived with her parents. It was actually her parent's party, so there was unlikely to be any really rowdy behaviour, half the guests being over 50. Obviously, from my perspective over-50s didn't misbehave.

I couldn't have been more wrong. There was so much drink on the kitchen table that I didn't imagine anybody would go home sober, especially if they drunk any of the punch which tasted as though it were nine parts vodka and one part fruit juice. Spliffs were openly passed round throughout the night and nobody blinked an eye. What went on on the cistern in the bathroom I didn't even dare *think* about.

It was a great party.

At one point during the evening I was walking into the kitchen when I heard someone mention Carl Demain's name. I stopped in my tracks, my empty glass in my hand, and listened.

From what I could gather of the conversation Carl Demain had been arrested. One of his so-called "buddies" had changed his story about playing poker with Demain on the night of the kidnap and had spilled the beans not only about that but also about Demain's involvement in other crimes, some even nastier and more socially unacceptable crimes than kidnapping. Demain was likely to be locked up for quite a while.

I rushed to find Nat, and found him sitting on the floor in the corner of the living room locked in an embrace with some blonde bimbo. I tutted – in the nicest possible way, of course, and headed back to the kitchen, a lighter spring in my step than had been there for some time. Demain being locked up was just what Russ needed, and it took some of the fear out of my heart.

Nat's 'blonde bimbo' turned out to be Nadine, someone who Nat knew because she often attended the band's gigs. She wasn't a bimbo at all as it turned out but was a solicitor, and, surprisingly, very nice. Nat introduced me to her later that evening and I told him about Demain's arrest.

"Oh, yes," Nadine said, "I know all about that, it's been the talk of anybody involved with the law all day."

She confirmed that what I'd heard was true, that Demain *had* been arrested, but it turned out that she didn't know 'all' about it at all. I had to wait for the next day to find out more.

Nadine came home with us – well, with Nat really, but we shared a cab. Nat was quite subdued, not in a sulky, miserable way, but not as leery as he sometime got when he'd downed a few beers, and not as loud in a show-offishy kind of way as he often was in front of a new girlfriend. I got the feeling that Nadine might be something different to his usual conquests and might, in time, turn out to be something quite special.

That was confirmed the next day, when Nat called round mid-morning. Apart from anything else it was unusual to see him up and about at that time of day, but he'd got up with Nadine, made her breakfast (muffins and coffee no doubt) and walked her to work.

"She's really nice," he told me. "Did you like her?"

I told him that on such a short acquaintance it was impossible to make a proper judgement and anyway, my judgement seemed a bit flawed but yes, I had found her really pleasant.

"I've known her for ages," he went on, "she's often at the gigs and we often chat quite a bit.

"I'm surprised you've never asked her out," I said, "she's very attractive."

In truth she was exactly the sort of girl – looks wise at least – that Nat normally went for. Sleek blonde hair fringing cornflower blue eyes, pert nose and sensuous lips. She was quite short and very, very slim. I'd hated her on sight but only in the way of women everywhere who feel they are a bit overweight and not startlingly pretty. Anyway, once I got talking to her I'd found her very likeable and intelligent and interesting.

"Thought she was too good for me," Nat admitted. "Didn't think she'd be interested in me at all, but it turns out that the reason she came to so many gigs was because she really fancied me."

"Lots of chemistry," I said and he nodded.

"She's terrific," he said, "Tonight we're going to the theatre."

"Really? That'll be a culture shock for you."

"No it won't," he said, "I was brought up in the theatre. Well, not literally, but mum and I used to go once a month, and I loved it."

"I didn't know," I said, and realised how little I really knew about him. Back home I knew my friends inside out, knew their parents and knew the sort of upbringing they'd had. I supposed if I stayed in Alaska I'd gradually get to know more about Nat's background and would eventually know him as well as my English friends. Friendships are built and grow on shared experiences and memories.

I made Nat a coffee and then he went back to his own apartment to tidy up. That was another change for the better. Nat's place was never a tip, but neither did he actually make a habit of specifically "tidying up", so it was usually comfortable, but a bit scruffy. I was sorry that I was not going to be here long enough to benefit from the change in my friend.

That afternoon there was a knock on the door and I opened it to find Russ standing there, Nat at his elbow.

"Let us in, hun," Nat said, looking anxiously over his shoulder.

My stomach churned. What had happened now? But when I looked closer neither of them looked *really* worried, so I stood aside and they hurried into the flat and stood and watched while I closed and locked the door. I didn't think I'd ever feel safe enough even in Cindy's apartment to *not* lock the door.

"You'd better sit down," I said. "Coffee?"

"Please, hun."

"Can I take it," I said, as I walked into the kitchenette, "that this *is* Russ, Nat? That this *is* the person who had my apartment before me."

"It is. This is the genuine article."

"I told you I was." Russ spoke for the first time.

"But you couldn't blame me for being cautious, could you?" I said as I made the coffee and carried two mugs through and put them on the occasional table. Going back into the kitchen I made my own drink and went and sat in the living area with them. "So what's been happening?" I asked. Nat and Russ were on the sofa, Russ's outdoor clothes slung over the back of it, so I took the armchair – Cindy's apartment was rather better furnished than the one I'd been renting.

"Good news, I think," Nat told him, and Russ shot him a look.

"It's *my* story," he said, but not unkindly, "so *I'll* tell it."

Nat grimaced. "The floor's yours, pal."

"As you know, Laura," Russ said, "I approached the cops down in Juneau and they were very interested. They took it higher, if you know what I mean, and it turned out there was already some suspicion about the team here in town. And also about Carl Demain's story. Anyway, one of his buddies that he was supposed to be playing poker with was arrested for his part in a drug smuggling gang. Seems he did a deal with the authorities and not only shopped his "buddy" Demain for the kidnapping but for one or two other things as well. If all goes to plan then Demain will get quite a long custodial sentence."

I sat back on the sofa and let out a long breath. "That's such good news," I said.

"I'll say," Russ said. I can't relax entirely, which is why I was anxious to get inside and not loiter on the landing, but the main threat has gone." He picked up his coffee. "I don't know what instructions Demain will leave with his sidekicks," he said, "There's no point now in trying to get the pictures from me though, not now the police have copies, but he might be out for revenge."

"So what will you do?" I asked.

He shrugged. "Emigrate. I'm getting married soon and then Siobhan and I are leaving the country. Forgive me if I don't tell you where I'm going; the less people that know the safer I – and they, will be." He stood up. "I just wanted you to know what was happening as you seem to have unwittingly become involved in this."

"Will the police want to talk to me?" I asked.

"I'm not sure," he said, putting on his coat, "but I wouldn't think so. There's nothing you can add unless it's anything about that Sara you told me about."

Sara. I'd forgotten about her. Would she be arrested, I wonder? Had she actually done anything wrong?

Russ said goodbye and I wished him luck and he left my life forever.

Six weeks later I left Alaska. I'd spent the previous evening with Nat and Nadine. I'd got to know Nadine really well since New Year's Eve and she was brilliant. Like Cindy, she had two personas. Well, like most of us, I suppose. When she was at work she wore severe black suits with white blouses, little pearl earrings and her hair in a neat bun. Out of work she wore her hair loose, and was either in jeans and jumper or long, floaty skirts and frilly tops. She was a barrel of laughs, drunk like a fish but never seemed the worse for wear, liked pop music and Beethoven, loved the theatre and the cinema but would never go inside a museum. "Too fuddy-duddy" she'd say, and wouldn't be talked into giving herself the opportunity to change her mind.

She and Nat were really an item now and saw each other whenever Nat wasn't gigging, and often when he was. One of Nat's songs was just shooting up the charts and was promising to make Nat a bundle of money and possibly a household name.

Cindy and Tony were well. Cindy had a part time job as a computer operator and in her spare time was doing dressmaking – another talent I was unaware of.

The girls at work were surprisingly – and gratifyingly - sad that I was leaving, given that I'd only been there a year. They had treated me to a great night out. Fifteen of us virtually took over a local diner and we stuffed ourselves silly before heading on to a night-club where we drunk until dawn. Then they put me in a taxi with a pile of farewell gifts and sent me home.

I saw Glen once. Sitting in a doorway, an upturned hat in front of him. "Spare a dollar for a cup of coffee, Miss?" he asked without looking up. I took a ten dollar note from my purse and threw it in the hat, then hurried away in case he looked up and saw who had been so generous.

I packed up a tea chest full of gifts and clothes and arranged for it to be shipped home. Hopefully I wouldn't be home too long before it joined me. I'd kept just enough that I could pack in a suitcase.

Con had repaired the door and its surround to my flat, had put down a new carpet and replaced the sofa! Somehow I wasn't surprised. I could see now that I'd been a mug to take on the apartment in the state it was in, but I'd been desperate. There was a middle-aged man living there now. We passed the time of day if we passed on the stairs but we didn't socialise apart from that. He kept himself to himself.

I didn't have to worry about him anyway. For one thing he looked like someone who could look after himself and for another Demain had been locked up and would be remaining behind bars for a good 10 years, even given time off for good behaviour.

The chief of the local police had been given a custodial sentence as well, it turned out he was Demain's cousin, and had as many fingers as Demain in illegal pies.

I hadn't heard from Sara. The police had come and interviewed me about my relationship with her and my visit to her parent's house but said that I wouldn't be required to attend court as a witness. The guy who'd posed as her father was also given a custodial, although not as long as Demain.

I tried to phone Sara once. I don't know why, just curiosity I suppose. Her number was unobtainable.

Nat drove me to the airport. Nadine didn't come. She said Nat had been on his own when I first met him and that he should be on his own when I left, which I thought was rather sweet of her. It wasn't true, of course, Nat hadn't been alone since I'd met him, there'd always been a girl or two hanging around, but I knew what she meant.

I checked in and then Nat and I went and had a coffee in the airport café. "Gonna miss you, hun," he said.

"Aw, Nat, that's sweet. I put a hand on his arm. "Believe it or not, I'm going to miss you too."

"I should bloody well hope so. Who's gonna brighten your day up now?"

Lots of people, actually, Nat. But I didn't say that. I told him that my life just wouldn't be the same without him in it, which, in a way, was true.

"But you'll keep in touch, won't you?" he asked anxiously. "You'll email? You know I can't write, so stick to emails."

When he said he couldn't write he meant he couldn't write letters, not couldn't actually write; he knew that I knew what he meant, we hadn't been friends for that long but somehow we knew each other pretty well.

"Yes, I'll email, Nat. You know I will. I've got your addy not only written in my diary and my notebook but it's engraved in my heart."

"I've got yours anyway," he said, "so I'll email you and then all you'll need to do is reply to it."

"I do know how to use email, Nat," I reminded him.

"I know you do, hun."

We sat in silence while we finished our drinks, then I looked at my watch. "Time to go," I said quietly.

He looked at me, his dark eyes gazing into mine as though committing my face to his memory. We both stood up and he took me in his arms. "Gonna miss you, hun," he said again.

He kissed me on my forehead, took my hand and led me to the departure gate. "Take care, and have a good life," he said, letting my hand drop from his.

"You too, Nat," I said, "And thanks for being such a great pal."

"You're welcome, m'lady." He did a kind of salute, clicked his heels together and turned away. I too, turned and went through customs. I didn't look back.

As I waited for my flight to be called I felt a growing sadness. Suddenly I wondered if I was doing the right thing. I'd given up my job and leaving some real friends behind me. But then I thought of home and knew that yes, this was right. I'd met some wonderful people in Alaska, but there were people back in England who would throw their arms round me and let me know where I belonged. Despite the happenings of recent months I'd had some great times in this country, but the good experiences I'd had in England outnumbered them by far.

Convinced, I turned my thoughts to home.

Home. Such a magical word. I couldn't wait.